D0030001

MISADVENTURES

WITH A

ROCK STAR

BY
HELEN HARDT

NO LONGER PROPERTY OF
ANYTHINK LIBRARIES/
RANGEVIEW LIBRARY DISTRICT

MISADVENTURES

WITH A
ROCK STAR

BY
HELEN HARDT

WATERHOUSE PRESS

This book is an original publication of Waterhouse Press.

This is a work of fiction. Names, characters, places, and
incidents either are the product of the author's imagination or
are used fictitiously, and any resemblance to actual persons,
living or dead, business establishments, events, or locales is
entirely coincidental. The publisher does not assume any
responsibility for third-party websites or their content.

Copyright © 2018 Waterhouse Press, LLC
Cover Design by Waterhouse Press.
Cover images: Shutterstock

All Rights Reserved.
No part of this book may be reproduced, scanned, or
distributed in any printed or electronic format without
permission. Please do not participate in or encourage piracy
of copyrighted materials in violation of the author's rights.
Purchase only authorized editions.

PRINTED IN THE UNITED STATES OF AMERICA

ISBN: 978-1-947222-15-1

For all the rock stars who have inspired me—
Chrissie Hynde, Ann Wilson, Pat Benatar, and
especially Joan Jett, plus many, many more!
It's always been my secret dream
to be up on stage with you.

CHAPTER ONE

JETT

Janet and Lindy tongued each other in a sloppy, openmouthed kiss. Lindy, platinum-blond with fair skin, smoothed her hand over the strap of ebony-haired Janet's soft-pink camisole before pulling it down and freeing one of her plump, dark tits. Her nipple was a deep violet, and Lindy skimmed her fingers over its tip before giving it a pinch.

Janet let out a low moan, sucked Lindy's bottom lip into her mouth, and released her creamy tits from the scant blue tube top she wore. They kissed each other more frantically, groaning, pinching and twisting each other's nipples.

"That's hot, man," Zane said, stroking the bulge under his jeans.

Zane Michaels was the keyboardist for our band, Emerald Phoenix. I loved him like a brother, but he hadn't matured past his teen years. I couldn't deny the ladies looked great, but this wasn't anything I hadn't witnessed many times before.

Lindy was now nestled between Janet's firm thighs, her pink tongue sliding between the folds of Janet's purple pussy. Zane looked about to explode.

And I couldn't have cared less.

Oh, Janet and Lindy were hot as hell. I'd had them separately and together, and they both gave killer blowjobs and let me fuck not only their pussies but their tight asses as well. Janet loved to be handcuffed to the bed, and Lindy let me spank her as hard as I liked.

Tonight, though? I wasn't interested.

Same old, same old.

I still had my post-performance high, but I wasn't looking for the usual orgy, despite Janet and Lindy's show and the rest of the scantily clad groupies milling around looking for attention. A redhead was perched on the lap of Bernie Zopes, our drummer, and the backup guitarist, Tony Walker, was getting a BJ from two women who looked like they might be twins.

Nah, couldn't be.

I'd already pushed a few hotties away after one shoved her tongue into my mouth and grabbed my crotch.

"What's with you, man?" Zane had asked.

I hadn't given him a response.

Truthfully, I didn't have one. I just wasn't in the mood. Not for this, anyway.

Zane passed me the joint he was smoking, but I waved it away. I no longer smoked. Bad for my voice. I'd already turned down his flask as well as the many drinks and drugs offered by the chicks in attendance. No booze. Not tonight. And I didn't do anything harder than that.

Not in the fucking mood.

One more concert, and one more drug- and booze- and groupie-filled after-party.

If anyone had told me five years ago I'd be tired of this scene, I would have laughed in his face.

Now?

Janet and Lindy finished their show and stood. Janet strode to Zane and unbuckled his belt, while Lindy walked toward me.

"Hey, Jett. You have way too many clothes on." She cupped my crotch, my lack of erection apparent. "Not happy to see me tonight?"

"Nothing personal, sweetheart. Just not in the mood."

"I always did love a challenge." She nipped at my neck.

"This isn't a challenge."

She pulled back and glared at me with her dark-blue eyes. "*Everything's* a challenge. I want you tonight, and I'm going to have you." She snaked her tongue over my bottom lip.

Well, what the hell? Fucking Lindy was no hardship, and I didn't have anything else pressing to do. My groin began to tighten.

But was it because of the blonde grinding on me? Or the auburn-haired, brown-eyed goddess I caught a glimpse of across the room?

CHAPTER TWO

HEATHER

Several hours earlier...

"I know you love this band," Susie said. "Come on. Please?"

Susie was my roommate and a good friend, but she was a notorious rock and roll groupie. The woman had a pube collection, for God's sake. She'd sworn me to secrecy on that one. She hadn't needed to bother. Who the heck would I tell? Pubic hair didn't regularly come up in conversation. Also, keeping locks of rock stars' gorilla salad in zippered bags made me kind of sick. I'd turned her down when she offered to show it to me.

"Sorry, Suze. Just not up for it tonight."

"I'm so sorry Rod Hanson turned down your rewrite. But sitting around wallowing in self-pity on a Friday night won't make it any better."

"And going to a concert will?"

"A concert *and* an after-party. And watching Jett Draconis and Zane Michaels on stage is an experience every woman should have at least once."

I did love Emerald Phoenix's music, and yes, Jett Draconis

and Zane Michaels were as gorgeous as Greek gods. But...

"Not tonight."

She pulled me off the couch. "Not taking no for an answer. You're going."

◆ ◆ ◆ ◆

Why was I here again?

I stifled a yawn. Watching a couple of women do each other while others undressed, clamoring for a minute of the band's attention, wasn't my idea of a good time. The two women were gorgeous, of course, with tight bodies and big boobs. The contrasts in their skin and hair color made their show even more exotic. They were interesting to watch, but they didn't do much for me sexually. Maybe if I weren't so exhausted. I'd pulled the morning and noon shifts, and my legs were aching.

Even so, I was glad Susie had dragged me to the concert, if only to see and hear Jett Draconis live. His deep bass-baritone was rich enough to fill an opera house but had just enough of a rasp to make him the ultimate rock vocalist. And when he slid into falsetto and then back down to bass notes? Panty-melting. No other words could describe the effect. Watching him had mesmerized me. He lived his music as he sang and played, not as if it were coming from his mouth but emanating from his entire body and soul. The man had been born to perform.

A true artist.

Which only made me feel like more of a loser.

Jett Draconis was my age, had hit the LA scene around the same time I had, and he'd made it big in no time. Me? I was still a struggling screenwriter working a dead-end job waiting tables at a local diner where B-list actors and directors hung out. Not only was I not an A-lister, I wasn't even serving them. When I couldn't sell a movie to second-rate producer Rod Hanson? I hadn't yet said the words out loud, but the time had come to give up.

"What are you doing hanging out here all by yourself?"

Susie's words knocked me out of my barrage of self-pity. For a minute anyway.

"Just bored. Can we leave soon?"

"Are you kidding me? The party's just getting started." She pointed to the two women on the floor. "That's Janet and Lindy. Works every time. They always go home with someone in the band."

"Only proves that men are pigs."

Susie didn't appear to be listening. Her gaze was glued on Zane, the keyboardist, whose gaze was in turn glued on the two women cavorting in the middle of the floor. She turned to me. "Let's make out."

I squinted at her, as if that might help my ears struggling in the loud din. I couldn't possibly have heard her correctly. "What?"

"You and me. Kiss me." She planted a peck right on my mouth.

I stepped away from her. "Are you kidding me?"

"It works. Look around. All the girls do it."

"I'm not a girl. I'm a thirty-year-old woman."

"Don't you think I'm hot?" she asked.

"Seriously? Of course you are." Indeed, Susie looked great with her dark hair flowing down to her ass and her form-fitting leopard-print tank and leggings. "So is Angelina Jolie, but I sure as heck don't want to make out with her. I don't swing that way." Well, for Angelina Jolie I might. Or Lupita Nyong'o. But that was it.

"Neither do I—at least not long-term. But it'll get us closer to the band."

"Is this what you do at all the after-parties you go to?"

She giggled. "Sometimes. But only if there's someone as hot as you to make out with. I have my standards."

Maybe I should have been flattered. But no way was I swapping spit with my friend to get some guy's attention. They were still just men, after all. Even the gorgeous and velvet-voiced Jett Draconis, who seemed to be watching the floor show.

Susie inched toward me again. I turned my head just in time so her lips and tongue swept across my cheek.

"Sorry, girl. If you want to make out, I'm sure there's someone here who will take you up on your offer. Not me, though. It would be too...weird."

She nodded. "Yeah, it would be a little odd. I mean, we live together and all. But I hate that you're just standing here against the wall not having any fun. And I'm not ready to go home yet."

I sighed. This was Susie's scene, and she enjoyed it. She had come to LA for the rockers and was happy to work as a receptionist at a talent agency as long as she made enough money to keep her wardrobe in shape and made enough contacts to get into all the after-parties she wanted. That was the extent of her aspirations. She was living her dream, and she'd no doubt continue to live it until her looks gave out... which wouldn't happen for a while with all the Botox and plastic surgery available in LA. She was a good soul, but right now her ambition was lacking.

"Tell you what," I said. "Have fun. Do your thing. I'll catch an Uber home."

She frowned. "I wanted to show you a good time. I'm sorry I suggested making out. I get a little crazy at these things."

I chuckled. "It's okay. Don't worry about it."

"Please stay. I'll introduce you to some people."

"Any producers or directors here?" I asked.

"I don't know. Mostly the band and their agents, and of course the sound and tech guys who like to try to get it on with the groupies. I doubt any film people are here."

"Then there isn't anyone I need to meet, but thanks for offering." I pulled my phone out of my clutch to check the time. It was nearing midnight, and this party was only getting started.

"Sure I can't convince you to stay?" Susie asked.

"Afraid not." I pulled up the Uber app and ordered a ride. "But have a great time, okay? And stay safe, please."

"I always do." She gave me a quick hug and then lunged toward a group of girls, most of them still dressed, thank God.

I scanned the large room. Susie and her new gaggle of friends were laughing and drinking cocktails. A couple girls were slobbering over the drummer's dick. The two beautiful women putting on the sex show had abandoned the floor, and the one with dark skin was draped between the legs of Zane Michaels, who was, believe it or not, even prettier than she was. The other sat on Jett Draconis's lap.

Zane Michaels was gorgeous, but Jett Draconis? He made his keyboardist look average in comparison. I couldn't help staring. His hair was the color of strong coffee, and he wore it long, the walnut waves hitting below his shoulders. His eyes shone a soft hazel green. His face boasted high cheekbones and a perfectly formed nose, and those lips... The most amazing lips I'd ever seen on a man—full and flawless. I'd gawked at photos of him in magazines, not believing it was possible for a man to be quite so perfect-looking—beautiful and rugged handsome at the same time.

Not that I could see any of this at the moment, with the blonde on top of him blocking most of my view.

I looked down at my phone once more. My driver was still fifteen minutes away. Crap.

Then I looked up.

Straight into the piercing eyes of Jett Draconis.

CHAPTER THREE

JETT

Eye contact.

She was beautiful in a toned-down way. While the other women at the party were dressed in tight clothes showing lots of cleavage, she wore a pink blouse, capri jeans, and simple black sandals. Her reddish hair was tied back in a high ponytail.

Definitely toned down.

And that was what struck me.

Those gorgeous eyes widened just a bit, and then she glanced down at her phone while turning and walking away.

My cock reacted.

Lindy had unbuttoned my shirt and was nibbling on my chest. She palmed my hard-on. "There's the Jett I know and love."

Problem was, the erection wasn't for her. I could make it work if I had to, but the beautiful woman walking away was pulling at me to follow.

I had to meet her. Had to get to her before she got away.

I nudged Lindy off of me. "Hey, sweetheart, I need to go."

"Go? What do you mean?"

"I mean I need to go. I'm sorry."

I stood, and she tumbled off me. I wasn't rude. Not usually. But blind determination swept through me. I had to meet this woman. Besides, Lindy wouldn't go home alone. Not with all the horny dick available in this room. She would be happy to show any of them a good time. I wasn't anything special to her. Already she was headed toward Zane and Janet.

Though my legs wanted to run, I walked steadily toward the exit and looked around. No sign of the woman. I raced through the concert hall and outside to the street.

She stood under a streetlight, waiting.

I walked toward her, though I had no idea what I'd say when I approached her.

"Hey."

Damn. I wrote Grammy-winning lyrics, and all I could come up with was "hey?"

She looked up. God, her eyes were beautiful. Big and deep-set, and the warmest brown I'd ever seen, like milk chocolate. I heated all over just looking at her, and my cock started to respond as well. I held myself in check. I didn't want to frighten her.

"Uh...hi," she said.

"Need a lift?" I asked.

She looked over her shoulder and then back at me, meeting my gaze. "Are you talking to me?"

I chuckled. "Who else would I be talking to, beautiful?"

Her cheeks flushed under the harsh glow of the streetlight, and her hair looked even redder. Was she a true redhead? I shifted my gaze down her gorgeous rack to her crotch. Or maybe she shaved or waxed. Maybe that pretty pussy was right beneath her jeans.

"My ride is coming."

"Who's picking you up?"

"Uber."

"I can do better than that. I'll take you home in my limo." I smiled.

She fidgeted with her phone. "I...can't."

"Why not?"

"For one, I don't know you."

I held out my hand. "I'm Jett. Jett Draconis."

Her cheeks reddened further. "I know that."

"Then you *do* know me."

"You know what I mean. I'm not a groupie. I don't just get into limos with rock stars."

"I know you're not a groupie."

"You do?"

"I've seen a lot of groupies, beautiful. You couldn't be less of a groupie if you had 'I'm not a groupie' tattooed on your forehead."

That got a cute little laugh out of her. "That obvious, huh?"

"So obvious. Since you're not a groupie, what were you doing at the party?"

"My roommate brought me. She *is* a groupie."

"Ah. I see. You know what?"

"What?"

"This conversation would be a lot more comfortable in the back of my limo."

She let out a huff. "I'm not going to have sex with you in your limo."

"Who said anything about sex?"

Her cheeks morphed from pink to deep red. "You said the back. I just thought..."

"Would you believe I'm not that kind of guy?"

"Not for a minute."

I couldn't fault her observation. I'd bedded my share of starlets and groupies—not to mention a certain cougar heiress I was sick to death of and had grown to despise—but the scene had gotten boring.

"Your face is all over the magazines and tabloids with someone new on your arm each time."

"Publicity, beautiful. That's all it is." Which was actually mostly the truth.

"You mean you don't sleep with all those women?"

"I didn't say that," I teased.

"Seriously? You get publicity photos with women and then take them to bed?" She shook her head as a small brown sedan drove up. "Brown Ford Fusion. My Uber's here. See you."

"No, wait." I grabbed her arm. "Let me take you home. Please."

"I don't think so."

"I don't sleep with them. Not *all* of them."

She unlatched the car door. "I'm Heather," she said to the driver as she slid into the backseat. Then she shut the door.

Heather.

Heather with the dark auburn hair and warm brown eyes.

Heather, who had just turned me down.

Turned down Jett Draconis, lead singer and guitarist for

Emerald Phoenix. Grammy winner. Voted sexiest rocker two years in a row.

Myriad groupies waited for me upstairs at the party. I could easily sate the granite hard-on I was sporting with one of them. Or two. Or three.

I raced back up.

CHAPTER FOUR

HEATHER

My heart was pounding like a snare drum. I'd known Jett Draconis was gorgeous, but when he stood right in front of my eyes, the moonlight streaking his dark hair with reddish highlights and his hazel eyes staring straight into mine... The man was the most beautiful thing I'd ever seen. That sculpted face, those full, dusky lips...

Sex emanated from him, from every pore in his body. His eyes spoke of lust. Or maybe that had been wishful thinking on my part.

Susie would have peed her pants if she'd known Jett had propositioned me.

Even more so if she knew how much I'd wanted to take him up on it.

But Heather Myles was a good girl. A sensible girl. She didn't get into limos with strange men—even famous and magnificent strange men who made her lady parts throb when she watched them onstage.

They'd throbbed even more when he'd stood in front of me in the street a few minutes ago.

He was still someone I didn't know. He could be a rapist.

No. Jett Draconis was no rapist. I wasn't sure how I knew, but I did. It was his eyes. He had kind eyes. Kind, sexy eyes.

Maybe I just needed to get laid. It had been a couple months, and I hadn't had a serious relationship in years. Why else would I have been so tempted to hop in Jett's limo and go with him to ecstasy?

And he *would* have taken me to ecstasy. Anyone who emanated sex the way he did would know exactly what buttons to push on my neglected body.

"Here you go," the driver said.

"Awesome. Thanks." I added a nice tip for him on the app and left the car.

Our apartment was garden level because it was cheaper. I did okay, and so did Susie, but she needed to support her groupie lifestyle, and I was hardly a spendthrift. Rather, I was a fanatic about saving money. At least we each had our own bedroom. The understated apartment complex was home mostly to struggling actors and writers, like myself, trying to make it in LA.

I wasn't a big drinker, but I poured myself a glass of Sauvignon Blanc and sat down on the worn couch in our small living area.

My nipples strained against my bra. How might Jett's full lips feel on them? I closed my eyes and trailed my fingers over the silk of my blouse, circling one nipple.

Another sip of wine.

I could go to my bedroom, but why? I was comfortable here, and Susie wouldn't be home for hours, if she came home at all tonight. I continued to finger my nipples as they budded against the two layers of fabric.

More. I wanted more. I took a third sip of wine and then set the goblet on the end table next to the sofa. I unbuttoned my blouse slowly until the two sides parted. I unclasped my bra in the back and lifted it over my breasts.

They fell gently against my flesh, my nipples protruding. I skimmed my fingers lightly over the skin of my chest and then zeroed in on my hard nipples. I closed my eyes and began playing with them, gently at first, and then twisting harder. My skin flushed with warmth, and a tingle shot between my legs.

Jett Draconis's face emerged in my mind, his full lips turning up into a smile. Mmm...yes, those lips kissing my nipples, sucking them, and when I could no longer stand it...a lustful bite.

I sucked in a breath, squeezed both my breasts lightly, and then trailed a hand down my abdomen to unbutton my jeans.

My panties were wet. I could already feel the moisture. I swept my tongue over my lips as I pushed my hand beneath my panties and found my clit. With my other hand, I continued to pinch one nipple.

An aroma rose in the air, the earthy scent signaling my arousal. I inhaled, letting it infuse me with a fiery warmth.

I dipped my fingers farther and smoothed the wetness over my folds, bringing it up to lubricate my clit. Jett's fingers. If only they were inside me, massaging my G-spot while he tugged on my nipples with those amazing lips.

Yes, there it was. I rubbed at my pussy, stroked my clit, pulled on my hard nipple... Until...

Until...

The orgasm pulsated through me, and I let out a low moan, undulating my hips against the worn fabric of the couch. I sank into the pleasure, oblivious to the sounds around me.

Then—

"Hey, Heather, are you still up?" A gasp. "Oh, shit!"

My eyes popped open.

Susie stood inside the door, and behind her...

God, just kill me now.

Jett Draconis.

CHAPTER FIVE

JETT

Heather. My auburn-haired goddess. And her tits were out. Luscious and swollen, as if they were waiting for me. Her jeans were unzipped, and the smell of lush female musk hung in the air.

I couldn't help inhaling.

A gentleman would have looked away.

No one would mistake me for a gentleman.

I regarded her, smiling, as she hurriedly put herself to rights. A shame to cover up such beauty.

"God, Heather," Susie said. "I'm so sorry."

"What are you doing home?" Heather asked between clenched teeth.

"Well...uh....Jett here... He wanted to meet you."

Heather's warm brown eyes took on a decidedly icy glare amidst her red cheeks. Were they red from embarrassment? Or from the climax she'd clearly just given herself? Had she been thinking of me?

"Oh?" Her voice cracked.

I wasn't sure what to say. I'd heard Heather tell the Uber driver her name, and she'd said her roommate was upstairs at the party, so I'd gone back up and bothered every girl there until I found the one with an auburn-haired roommate named Heather. It hadn't taken long to convince Susie to take a limo ride to her small apartment so I could meet her elusive friend.

"I'm so sorry, Heather." Susie looked toward the ceiling.

"It's my fault," I said. "I forced her to bring me here."

"Forced?" Heather's tone was acidic.

"No, of course not," Susie said. "He wanted to meet you, and I *agreed* to bring you here."

"You brought a stranger to our apartment at"—I glanced at the cable box—"one forty-five a.m.?"

"Jett's not a stranger," Susie said.

"Oh. He's a *friend* of yours?" Her tone was still caustic.

Many years had passed since I'd felt like I didn't belong somewhere. Most people in LA welcomed me with open arms, happy to get an autograph or a selfie with me. But not Heather.

And that only made me want her more.

Her skin was flushed rose, and she'd misbuttoned her shirt. I couldn't help smiling. She was fucking adorable.

I cleared my throat. "I didn't mean to intrude." Yeah, that was a lie. I totally meant to intrude. "You want to go get a drink or something?"

"It's almost two a.m."

"Yeah. In LA. So what?"

"I have to work tomorrow."

"Not until the dinner shift," Susie offered.

Heather darted her gaze to Susie, a slight frown marring her beauty. "I'm not dressed to go out."

"You look great to me." God, she did. I'd underestimated

how hot her body might be. That rack of hers was extraordinary.

"This is insane," she said. "You had your pick of hot women at the party. Why are you here, really? Because I told you I'm not a groupie."

"Yeah. I know."

"Heather," Susie said, "you're being kind of rude. And what's wrong with being a groupie?"

"No offense," Heather said. "But that's not the life for me."

"I'm not asking you to suck my dick, sweetheart," I said jovially. "I'm asking you to have a drink with me."

Heather winced. Only slightly, but I noticed. I'd probably been a little too brash.

"Hey, I'm sorry. But seriously, what's the harm in a drink?"

Susie strode toward her and grabbed her arm. "Are you crazy? I know you're a fan."

She was a fan? Good news. "So you're a fan, huh?"

She nodded slightly.

"You want an autograph? A selfie?"

She scoffed. "Or the privilege of sucking your dick, maybe?"

Not the right approach. She might be a fan, but she clearly wasn't a *fanatic*. I looked around the modest room. What Heather and Susie didn't know was that I'd once lived in this complex. Five years ago, when I first came to LA with Zane. We'd teamed up with Tony and Bernie shortly after, and Emerald Phoenix had been born...with a little help from a benefactor.

I closed my eyes and inhaled. So didn't want to go there right now. I didn't need to think about what I'd given up to become Jett Draconis.

"How long have you lived here?" I asked.

"I've been here a while," Susie said. "Heather moved in a couple years ago."

I nodded. Now what? I sure as hell wasn't leaving without what I'd come for.

And she was still glaring at me.

Time to soften up a little. I approached Heather and stroked my index finger along her silk-clad upper arm. Even through the fabric, I felt sparks. "Look. I just want to talk to you. Maybe get to know you. Would that be so horrible?"

"In the middle of the night?" She looked down.

I tipped her chin upward with my index finger. Her skin was so soft. "I'm awake. You're awake. You don't have to work until tomorrow evening, and neither do I. Sounds perfect."

She sucked her bottom lip into her mouth for a few delicious seconds. "Just because you walked in on me...you know...doesn't mean I'm easy."

"Sweetheart, no one would ever mistake you for easy." Though I planned to hit a home run later. She just didn't know it yet.

"Okay. Let's have a drink."

My body relaxed. Man, I hadn't realized how tense I was, waiting for her to decide to come with me. I never got tense about women.

Weird.

"Why don't we have a drink here?" She pointed to a half-empty glass of wine on a nearby table. "I've already poured one for myself."

Susie's eyes brightened. She was attractive, but a threesome wasn't what I had in mind. I was pretty sure that wouldn't be Heather's jam either.

"We'll compromise," I said. "Come out to my limo. I have a fully stocked bar, and there's plenty of room. We won't go anywhere. We'll just have a drink." And there was plenty of room for other activities as well.

Susie frowned and then feigned a yawn. "I guess I'll hit the sack."

"Susie..." Heather pleaded.

"Look, either have a drink with him or don't, but I'm exhausted. Good night." She walked into one of the bedrooms.

Alone at last. "So?" I said.

She twisted her lips. "Why do you want to have a drink with me? You're not going to get anywhere."

"All I want is a drink, sweetheart."

"I have a name."

"All I want is a drink, Heather."

A smile curved her lips. Yes! She was starting to de-ice. "We don't move. We stay right here in front of my building."

"You got it, sweet— I mean Heather."

CHAPTER SIX

HEATHER

I must be out of my mind.

No, he must be out of his mind. What does he want with me when he has groupies galore screwing each other just to turn him on?

Jett said something to his driver that I couldn't hear and then opened the limo door for me. I got in and sat down on pure luxury—a bright-green leather bench that was as plush as any sofa in a five-star hotel lobby. Not that I'd seen a lot of five-star hotels in LA, but I'd been in a few for meetings. None of which had amounted to anything.

"This is amazing," I couldn't help gushing.

"I'm glad you like it. Green is kind of my color. You know, like purple was Prince's."

"I know. I love your green guitar. Is that how the band got its name?"

"Yeah. It was all a huge publicity thing when we first started out." He scooted to the bar, which had a golden marble countertop, complete with cup holders so nothing would spill if the limo was moving. "What's your pleasure?"

"White wine, I guess."

"Chardonnay? Pinot Grigio? Riesling?"

"Sauvignon Blanc."

"You got it." He opened a small refrigerator, took out a tiny bottle of wine, opened it, and poured it into a stemmed glass. "Here you go."

"What are you having?" I asked.

"Me? Just some mineral water."

"You don't drink?"

"Not as much as I used to. And I gave up smoking."

"You smoked?"

"Not cigarettes. They do too much vocal harm. But I smoked pot every now and then. I don't do that anymore either. Can't risk what pays the bills."

I stared at his neck. "Good call. You've got a gold mine right there."

"What?"

"I mean your voice. It's incredible. Truly."

"Thanks." He smiled. "So you *are* a fan."

"Of course. Your voice is amazing. So rich and full."

"I'm actually classically trained. Opera is my first love."

Though I'd had no idea, I wasn't overly surprised. I'd always thought his voice could fill an opera house. "Yeah? Where did you study?"

"Juilliard."

"No way!"

"Full scholarship. I got my master's at Northwestern in Chicago."

"You're kidding!"

"Nope. Why do you seem so surprised?"

"It's that...I got my master's at Northwestern too. In creative writing." Had we been there at the same time? Suddenly I was having trouble breathing. Jett was an educated man. Knock me over with a feather. "Why didn't you go into opera?"

"I couldn't get any jobs. People loved my voice, but said I was too young. My voice hadn't matured yet. Men's voices don't mature until they get well into their thirties."

"How'd you get into rock, then?"

"I've always loved rock and roll. I'm a big fan of the classics. Zane and I went to grad school together. He was a classical pianist with a vocal minor. We were both twenty-five at the time, and going nowhere in our chosen fields. We needed something to pay the bills, and we both refused to take day jobs."

"That was brave of you." Very brave. I wished I hadn't caved and taken a day job. Of course, if I hadn't, I'd be living on the streets. "Aren't you afraid rock will ruin your voice?"

"Nah. I know how to take care of my voice. It's all about singing healthy."

"I guess you learned all about that during your years at Juilliard and Northwestern. I never would have thought..."

"Never would have thought a dumb rocker like me could be educated at such fine institutions of higher learning?" Despite his words, his tone was jovial.

"I didn't mean—"

"Of course you did. I know I'm not taken seriously. Not like I would be if I were doing opera. It's part of the price I paid, and I'm good with it."

"No, really, I—"

"I got a perfect score on my ACT, by the way. There *are* brains in this head."

"If you'd let me finish a sentence, please!" I'd been one point away from a perfect ACT score myself, a point that had always irked me, but never more so than at this moment. "I'm sorry. I didn't mean to imply that you weren't smart. I think anyone who has the kind of success you've had must be intelligent. You made all the right decisions."

"Or had them made for me," he said a bit more quietly.

"What do you mean?"

"Nothing." He took a long drink from his bottle of Evian. "I'd like to know about *you*."

I sipped my wine. "I'm a screenwriter."

"Yeah? What have you written? Maybe I've seen some of your movies."

Brick in gut. Nothing of mine had yet made it to the big screen. Hence, the day job. I tried to swallow down my embarrassment.

"I'm afraid I haven't sold any of my scripts yet." *Just shoot me now.* Whatever passing interest Jett had in me would quickly evaporate. Why would such a successful musician want anything to do with a loser who couldn't sell her stuff? A loser who had decided to throw in the towel.

"Really? How do you make a living, then?"

"I wait tables at Lucien's Diner."

He didn't seem fazed. "Where are you from? Where did you go for your undergrad?"

Way to change the subject to avoid any more

embarrassment on my part. It was actually nice of him. Almost chivalrous. "I'm from Chicago. I got my BA in creative writing at DePaul and then, of course, my MA at Northwestern."

"That's right. We're both masters." He smiled.

"On paper, anyway."

"You'll make it, Heather. Hey, I know someone—"

"I don't need any favors." What a lie. I *did* need a favor. But I already knew how Jett would want to be repaid.

Not that sleeping with him would be any hardship, and God...I hadn't been laid in forever.

But I was determined not to fall into that Hollywood trap.

"Who said anything about favors?" he said. "If you'd let me finish. I know a woman who's putting together a TV pilot, and she needs a writer. I could introduce you."

"TV?" I'd never given any thought to the small screen. But with so many cable networks now, plus digital networks, TV could be a good way to get my feet wet. Still...I so wanted to write movies.

"Yeah. It may seem smaller, but—"

"I'm not a diva. I want to write for the screen. Big or small." And I hadn't even known that until this very instant.

"Great. Her name is Laney Taylor. I'll set up a meeting."

Laney Taylor. Sounded lean and leggy. And she'd probably had Jett Draconis's cock in her mouth on more than one occasion. The thought was sobering. Why did I care where Jett kept his cock?

"What kind of show is she producing?"

He laughed. "I have no idea. I think it's a paranormal thing or something."

Paranormal? Not really my area. But if I got paid to write, I could write anything.

Sell out, sell out.

Shut up, little voice.

"Did you ever feel like you were selling out?" I asked, suddenly needing to know.

"Where did that come from?"

"I didn't mean it in a bad way. But you said you loved opera. Instead you went where the money is."

"Ha! There were no guarantees when Zane and I came to LA. Do you know how many struggling rockers are out there trying to get noticed? We got"—he hedged a bit—"lucky."

"But why—"

"I told you. I was too young to break into opera with my voice type. I wanted to sing, not sling hash somewhere."

He slid closer to me on the green leather bench. My heart jumped.

"Need a refresher?" He took my wine glass, which, oddly, was almost empty.

"No. I'm good."

"Good." He set the glass in one of the cup holders. "Because there's something *I* need."

CHAPTER SEVEN

JETT

I hadn't realized how stunning Heather—

What was her last name? And since when did I care about a woman's last name?

She swept her tongue slowly over her lower lip. And I about jizzed in my pants.

"What?" she asked.

"What's your name?" I said. "I mean, your last name."

"Myles. Heather Myles. With a Y, not an I."

I smiled. "Okay, Heather Myles with a Y. You want to know what I need?"

"Well...sure. I guess."

"I need *this*." I pressed my lips gently to hers.

A small sound of shock emerged from her throat, but then she parted her lips. Thank God. I took the invitation and swept my tongue into her warm mouth, finding hers. She tasted like the wine with some added sweetness. I explored the silk of her cheek with one hand and grasped her auburn ponytail with the other.

She pulled back. "What are you doing?"

"I was kissing you."

"You pulled my hair."

"I just wanted to touch it. It's so beautiful. It looks like a satin waterfall. I wanted to see what it felt like."

"Oh..." A smile twitched at her lips.

The old "hair like satin" line. Worked every time.

Problem was...I really meant it this time. Her hair *had* been gloriously soft and delicate against my fingers calloused from playing guitar.

Guitar wasn't even my first choice of instrument. Voice was, followed by piano. But I'd been doing all three since I was a kid.

I leaned toward her again, desperate to feel those perfect lips against mine.

But again, she pulled back. "I...can't do this."

"It's just a kiss, sweetheart."

"You don't stop with just a kiss. I saw what was going on at that party."

"Did you see *me* doing anything?"

"I saw that blond girl gyrating all over you."

"Key words there. *She* was gyrating. I wasn't."

"You didn't exactly push her away."

"Actually I did. Right after I watched you leave."

"Oh?"

This was getting old fast. I wanted this woman. Would I call her again after? Probably not. I'd get her out of my system just like I got all the others out of my system after a fuck. Problem was...most of the others didn't take this much convincing.

"Come on, Heather. Just kiss me. Your lips are so soft and

pink. I love how they felt against mine."

"Oh..." She closed her eyes.

I took that as a go-ahead. I traced her lips with my tongue and then gave her a soft kiss. When she opened, I went in slowly this time. She was the type of woman who required lots of warming up. That was okay. I could do that. Anything to get that sweet body naked and under me.

My cock was going crazy in my jeans. I wanted to tie her down and fuck her hard. Despite my instincts, I knew I had to take it slow with her.

With Heather.

Now that I said her name, I liked it. It flowed from my lips like fine Burgundy. Her tongue was like velvet against mine, and the kiss was...

Damn, it was just a kiss, but my cock was ready to explode. Without thinking, I grabbed her hand and planted it on my crotch.

She pushed me away, my lips ripping from hers.

"What the hell are you doing?"

What *had* I been doing? I'd already figured out what kind of woman she was. The kind who needed lots of warmup. Why had I gone crazy on her?

"Hey, I'm sorry. I just thought—"

"You just thought I'd fuck you. Right here in your limo. So much for 'just a drink.'" She scooted toward the door.

"Heather, wait. I'm sorry. I didn't mean—"

She fled out the door and slammed it in my face.

I sat back, frustrated.

Frustrated and...something else. An emotion I wasn't

familiar with.

Something like...loss?

Fuck that. I pushed the button for the intercom and told Lars to take me back to the after-party. I'd sate my desires there.

♦ ♦ ♦ ♦

About half the partiers had left for the night, but the festivities were still going. Lindy was still there, and she ran to greet me when I returned, Janet in tow.

"Jett! I'm so glad you came back."

"Hey, sweethearts," I said to them.

Janet curled her arms around my neck and kissed my cheek. "You look like you could use some attention."

"Baby, you got that right." I winked. "Why don't the three of us take this party out to my limo?"

CHAPTER EIGHT

HEATHER

For a minute—more like a microsecond—I'd thought Jett Draconis might be different. A Juilliard man. Someone who valued education. Who protected his most prized asset—his voice—as best he could.

Even after I'd found out he was just a typical celebrity lech, I still had trouble breaking away and leaving that limo.

He was magnificently gorgeous. That was all. Purely physical.

I didn't have time for physical.

Or did I?

My life had gotten stale—waiting tables, trying to stay awake when I was dead on my feet to keep my writing dream alive, meeting with producers, getting rejected...

Maybe physical was just what I needed.

Didn't matter, though. I'd blown my chance to have a one-nighter with the glory that was Jett Draconis.

What had I been thinking? I'd been perfectly safe. I was in a limo and I could have left at any time.

Oh, well...

I went to the bathroom, washed up, brushed my teeth, and

then headed back to my room for bed.

Only to find Susie sprawled on my blanket.

"So how was it?" she asked, her eyes wide.

"How was what?"

"Jett? He couldn't take his eyes off you. He was seriously freaked out when he found me at the party. He was desperate to find you."

"Desperate? I doubt Jett Draconis is ever desperate. He can have whoever he wants."

"Tonight he clearly wanted you. So how was it?"

"You think I hopped into the sack with him? I was gone all of half an hour."

"That's more than enough time for the good stuff."

"Suze, you know I don't sleep around."

"I know, I know." She rolled her eyes. "But this is Jett Draconis. Maybe he's not quite as pretty as Zane Michaels, but he's easily the second-best-looking man in rock and roll today. Plus, he's so talented, and a genuinely nice guy."

A sudden spear of jealousy lanced into my gut. "Suze, have you ever..."

"With Jett?" She shook her head. "I wish. I did engage in some heavy petting with Zane once, though. He's amazing."

I couldn't help smiling as relief swept through me. I wasn't sure why. I had no claims on Jett Draconis. I had just turned him down, after all. Susie had said Zane was prettier than Jett. Zane was blond and blue-eyed and had that Jon Bon Jovi look about him. But Jett... Jett was pure rugged maleness. Beautiful, but in an entirely masculine way.

"So seriously," she continued. "How was it?"

Clearly, Susie wasn't going to let this die.

"Seriously, Suze, I didn't go to bed with him."

Her eyes went wide with shock. "You mean nothing happened?"

A few kisses, but I didn't feel like talking about it. For some reason, it felt very private to me.

"I had a glass of wine. He had some water. We talked."

"About what?"

"Where he went to school."

"He went to school? You mean college?"

"Yeah. He has a master's in music. Didn't you know that?"

"I didn't. He really knows his stuff, though, so it's not surprising. I guess it just doesn't come up at the after-parties or clubs where I run into him."

You think? I kept my thoughts and feelings to myself. "So yeah, nothing happened, and I need to get to bed. It's three o'clock, and I have work tomorrow evening."

"Okay, okay. I can take a hint." She clambered off my bed. "Night."

"Night."

♦ ♦ ♦ ♦

"Broken Sky," written by none other than Jett Draconis, woke me from my slumber. I hadn't set an alarm. It was my ringtone. I grabbed my phone from the night table. Hmm. Didn't recognize the number.

I yawned and said, "Hello?"

"Good morning. I'm trying to reach Heather Myles," a female voice said.

"You found her."

"Oh, great! My name is Laney Taylor. I got your name from Jett Draconis. He said you're a television script writer?"

Well, not exactly. I had a bit of brain fog going on. Had she said TV script writer? I was a screenwriter. Of course, since none of my writing had actually made it to any screen, big or small, I guessed I was whatever I wanted to be.

I cleared my throat. "That's right. It's nice to hear from you."

"Jett called me first thing this morning and said amazing things about you and your work. He insisted I call you right away. I hope I'm not disturbing you so early on a weekend morning."

My mouth dropped open but no words emerged. Jett had said amazing things about me and my work? We'd shared all of a half hour together, and he had no idea what kind of writer I was.

"Are you there?"

Get it together, Heather. "Yeah, sorry."

"I'm so sorry. Did I wake you?"

"It's okay. I have to get up anyway. I had a late night last night. I'm thrilled to talk to you."

"Wonderful. Are you free for a drink tonight? I'd love to talk to you about my project."

Crap. "I'm sorry. I have to work the evening shift at Lucien's."

Damn it! My brain was half-assed right now. Why had I said that? I could have easily gotten my shift covered or called in sick. Now she'd think I wasn't a serious writer if I still had a day job.

"How about now, then?" she said. "We could catch a late lunch."

Except that I was still in bed with drool hanging off my chin. But I couldn't let this opportunity pass me by. "Sure. Just tell me when and where."

"How about the Brasserie on Vine? I have a standing table there. How soon can you get there?"

I desperately needed a shower, but I didn't want to show up with wet hair... Screw it. I'd wash the essentials, dab on a little makeup, and hope I didn't look like I'd only gotten a few hours of sleep.

"A half hour?" I said.

"Perfect. See you there." She ended the call.

I froze. What had I gotten myself into?

CHAPTER NINE

JETT

I woke to the noonday sun streaming in my bay window and rose to go to the bathroom. Janet and Lindy were a tangle of black and white arms and legs on my bed. They'd been so high. It would be a while before they got up.

My marble floor was cold beneath my bare feet. I walked naked to the toilet, took a piss, and then turned on the shower.

I'd had no problem getting a hard-on when Janet and Lindy had treated me to another one of their shows in my bedroom last night, but I hadn't let either of them touch me. After a bit of whining, I'd plied them with a few pieces of costume jewelry I had on hand and convinced them I was exhausted and just wanted to watch for the night.

After they'd given each other a few more orgasms, they'd both passed out in my bed. I'd actually slept in the lounge chair by my bay window. I'd thought about masturbating while they did each other—anything to relieve my massive hard-on—but something had stopped me.

Something in the form of Heather Myles.

That damned woman wouldn't get out of my head.

I let out a moan as the hot water whooshed out of the

shower head and onto my fatigued body. Live music was hard work. I feared my body was growing old before its time. Not my voice, though. I took care of that with kid gloves. One day I'd sing Mozart's *Figaro* at the Met. Then Javert in *Les Miz* on Broadway.

One day...

I closed my eyes and stood in the stream of steaming water, letting it gush all over me. Heather's lips popped into my mind. How amazing it had felt to kiss them, to feel her soft tongue against mine. My cock hardened between my legs, and I began stroking it as I imagined Heather's soft lips wrapping around it. A moan crept out of my throat as I fisted it more strongly.

"Need some help with that?"

I shot my eyes open. Lindy, stark naked, of course, had entered the shower. Her nipples stood straight out from her silicone breasts.

"What are you doing in here?"

"Just helping out where I'm needed." She sank to her knees and took my cockhead between her lips.

So she wasn't Heather. So she wasn't the woman whose face was in my fantasy. That didn't mean I couldn't get a kickass BJ in the shower. My eyes were closed. I had a good imagination. I could pretend it was Heather whose mouth was wrapped around my cock.

She began with tiny licks over the head and along the shaft. She slid her hands from my knees up my thighs and cupped my ass. Then she plunged her mouth down upon me, taking me nearly to my base. I'd had many blowjobs from Lindy. She was an expert at deep-throating.

Relax, I said to myself. *Just let it feel good. Imagine... Imagine...*

She continued her expert ministrations, but instead of relaxing, I tensed as the water continued to pelt me.

A few seconds later...my flaccid cock dropped from her mouth.

She looked up at me. "What's wrong, babe?"

What *was* wrong? Since when had I not been able to stay hard for a blowjob? Especially one as expertly performed as this one?

I gave her a halfhearted smile. "Sorry, sweetheart. I'm just really tired. Last night's concert took a lot out of me."

She stood and wrapped her arms around me. "You were a fucking rock star last night, no pun intended. It was one of the best performances I've ever seen."

Though I smiled, I knew she said similar things to every rocker she bedded. Those words would've meant so much more coming from someone who actually meant them.

Coming from Heather.

No use. Clearly, my cock wasn't going to work until it had its fill of Heather Myles. It happened to me every once in a while. I became ferociously attracted to a woman, and she was all I wanted. Once I bedded her, the craving subsided.

Since I didn't plan to go without sex for the rest of my life, there was only one solution available to me.

I had to get Heather Myles in my bed, and I had to do it soon.

"I've missed you, babe," Lindy was saying. "It's been ages

since you took me to your playground. We could go there now. Even if you're tired. I don't mind. You could use your toys on me."

My toys. Interesting. Lindy really didn't care whether *I* fucked her. She'd be happy being fucked by one of the dildos in my playroom. As long as a rock star was performing the action.

Man, the scene was getting old.

Zane had given me shit about this before. When I got my dick in a bunch about a particular woman, I'd tell him I was getting tired of the scene. I'd fuck her, get her out of my system, and then be right back in the middle of the scene as usual.

Surely that was all that was going on now. I'd have Heather Myles, and then I'd feel great.

"Sorry, sweetheart. The playroom's closed. Renovations."

That was a big lie, but I didn't care. I only wanted one woman in my playroom at the moment, and it wasn't Lindy or Janet. The problem was...I wasn't sure Heather Myles would ever consent to going into my playroom. She was a different kind of woman. I honestly didn't know what to expect from her.

Only one way to find out.

I turned the shower off, grabbed a towel, and handed another to Lindy. "Sweetheart, I think you and Janet need to be going. I've got lots of things to do before the concert tonight."

Lindy pouted. "We just wanted to have some fun, Jett."

"There will be another party tonight, and you two will be right back in business." I toweled off without looking at her. "I want you both gone by the time I'm out of the bathroom. Lars will take you wherever you need to go."

Lindy gave a *hmph* and walked out, slamming the door

behind her. I hadn't meant to sound so dismissive, but those two women meant nothing to me. Not that Heather Myles meant anything to me either, but until I had her soft pliable body under mine, I wasn't going to be any use to any other woman. I knew that much about myself.

I dressed in a pair of athletic shorts and a tank top, pulled my hair back into a loose ponytail, and decided to go for a run. Maybe that would help work some of the sexual frustration out of me.

Then I changed my mind and turned in the athletic shorts for an old pair of broken-in jeans. The sexual frustration might be eating me alive, but it would make for an amazing performance tonight. Instead, I'd go get lunch and a heaping cup of coffee.

I knew just the place. On Vine.

CHAPTER TEN

HEATHER

"So you haven't worked in television before?" Laney swirled the clear liquid of her martini before taking a sip.

How someone could drink a martini at one in the afternoon was beyond me, but this was LA.

"I'm afraid I haven't. I'm sorry if Jett led you to believe otherwise."

"No, he didn't say that at all. I just assumed, since he was recommending you so highly."

He was recommending me because he wants to get into my pants. He wants me to owe him a favor.

"It's so kind of him to speak highly of me, but we really don't know each other that well. We only met recently. But I do believe my work will speak for itself. I have some screenplays you could read, although they're feature-length."

"But none of them have been sold?"

"I've come close a few times, but unfortunately, no."

"That's perfectly all right. I believe in giving new talent a chance. After all, we all started at the bottom. Even the great Jett Draconis himself." She smiled.

"That's so kind of you. I appreciate you taking a look."

"Did you bring anything with you?"

"Of course. I always come prepared." I picked up the messenger bag that sat at my feet and pulled out two scripts that I considered to be my best work. "One of these is a romantic comedy, the other a drama. Jett told me your new project has a paranormal aspect. I'm afraid I don't have anything paranormal to share with you, but I do enjoy the genre and would love to have the chance to write something." So that was a little white lie. I had no familiarity with the genre, but as of today, I'd start scanning Netflix for good paranormal television shows to binge watch.

After all, I was a trained writer. I could learn to write anything.

I couldn't help smiling to myself at the thought. My conversation with Jett had been enlightening. I'd had no idea that he had a classical background and that opera was his first love. He had an amazing and hypnotizing rock and roll voice. Anyone who heard him in concert would think rock and roll was his true calling. But he'd gone where he thought he could sing for a living, and he'd found success.

Truthfully, the rocker hadn't been out of my mind since I laid eyes on him the night before. Of course, I had an intense physical attraction to him. What woman wouldn't? But after talking to him, if only for a short time, I'd felt a more intimate connection. The kisses we'd shared...

He had no idea how difficult it had been for me to leave that limo.

"...with a darker flare."

Crap. Laney had been talking to me, and I'd missed most

of what she had said because I've been daydreaming about a rock star.

I cleared my throat. "Pardon me?"

She took another sip of her drink. "I'm looking for something like *Buffy the Vampire Slayer* or *True Blood*, but with a darker flare."

I'd never watched either of those, but at least I'd heard of them.

"Not a lot of humor. A little would be okay, but mostly drama. I want to tackle some significant issues relating to violence."

"I see. Can you elaborate a bit?"

"I can, but I have a whole premise written up. I think it might be better for you to read that first. May I email it to you?"

"Of course." I pulled a business card out of my messenger bag and handed it to her. "My email and phone number are on there."

The waiter arrived with our lunches. I cut a bite off my chicken breast and had it halfway to my mouth when I stopped, frozen.

Heading toward us, wearing old beat-up jeans and a tank top, his dark hair pulled back—looking even more delicious than he had in his limo last night—was none other than Jett Draconis.

This was clearly the laid-back Jett, and oh boy, could he pull it off.

I zeroed in on his full lips first. They had just a touch of shine to them, making them irresistible. Then I slid my gaze to his upper arms. Not many guys could work a black wifebeater, but this one could. His shoulders were broad and muscled, his skin a light bronze, and on his left upper arm was a glorious tattoo. It wasn't a phoenix, for his band, or even a dragon, given his surname. No. It was a Celtic lion done all in black.

And because it wasn't expected, it was perfect.

His arms were magnificently sculpted with muscles and sinew. Even his hands were good-looking, with long, thick fingers and perfectly shaped square fingernails. Sculpted abs pressed through the tank, and his thighs...

Oddly, I hadn't visually assessed him in this manner last night. I'd concentrated on his face and hair. His face was magnificent no matter what, and right now his hair was pulled back. In the light of day, it was impossible not to notice everything about him. I scanned down his jeans to his feet, clad in basic flip-flops. My God, the man even had beautiful feet.

How was it possible for a person to be so glorious to look at and listen to at the same time?

The universe had been kind to this one. He was gifted with so much. Did he know how lucky he was?

He sauntered up to our table as if he belonged there. "Hey, ladies."

"Jett!" Laney's eyes glowed. "We were actually just talking about you."

Had we been? She had said Jett spoke highly of me. That hardly constituted "talking about him."

"Were you?" He smiled, obviously going into flirtation mode.

"We were. Please, join us," Laney cooed.

"Don't mind if I do." Instead of sitting next to Laney, he

took the seat next to me. "Hey there, Heather."

"Hi," was all I could get out.

"How's everything going?"

"Oh...fine."

"Isn't Laney the best?"

"Yes, she's great." I'd known her for about five minutes, but what else could I say?

"You're such a sweet talker, Jett," Laney said.

Then I saw it in her eyes—that indescribable look that said "Yes, I've fucked him."

Didn't go over so big with me.

Had this man slept with *every* woman in LA? I wouldn't have been surprised.

Laney's phone buzzed against the table and she picked it up. "I'm so sorry. Could you two excuse me for a minute? I need to take this."

"Of course," Jett said.

Laney stood, put the phone to her ear, and left the table.

While I sat twiddling my thumbs.

"Funny running into you here," Jett said.

"Yes. That is very funny, indeed."

"You don't seem amused."

"You knew I would be here. You gave Laney my name. You knew she would call me this morning."

"Now that's a new one. No one's ever told me I'm clairvoyant before."

I smiled without meaning to. Damn, he did have a great personality.

That, in conjunction with his intelligence, talent, and

godlike looks? How was I supposed to resist him?

"You're not."

Oh my God. Had I said that aloud? "I'm not what?"

"What? No, I said, 'you're welcome.'"

"Oh." Just when I thought he was so irresistible. Although I really should have thanked him. "I do appreciate you introducing me to Laney. And I am a polite person. I was getting to thanking you. Most people wait to say 'you're welcome' until after they're thanked."

"Sweetheart, I have never in my life been most people."

There he went with the sweetheart again. Funny, though. I kind of like how it sounded. But the fact that he'd probably called about a thousand other women sweetheart in the last year alone kind of negated it a little.

"So what do you think? About Laney's project?"

"I don't really know a lot about it yet. She's going to send me the premise and proposal via email."

"Yeah? So she's interested in you?"

"Only because you gave me such a great talk-up. But I gave her some of my work, and it will speak for itself."

"I'm sure it's brilliant."

"How can you be so sure? None of it has seen the light of day yet."

"Because, Heather, you're not a run-of-the-mill screenwriter looking for work. You're special."

Special? We'd spent all of half an hour together. Yeah, he was definitely trying to get into my pants. And I was probably going to let him. Problem was, I didn't want to be one more notch on Jett Draconis's bedpost. I actually *did* want to be special. Special to him.

I gave a brief thought to a sarcastic comment, but decided on "That's nice of you to say."

Laney came hurrying back. "I am so, so sorry, Heather. I have to go to an impromptu meeting right away. It simply can't be avoided." She looked down at her plate of chicken piccata and threw several twenty-dollar bills on the table. "That should cover lunch. Jett, I hope you're hungry. I didn't touch this." Then she turned to me. "I've got your card, Heather. I'll be in touch."

"Thank you so much for meeting with me." I gave her the best smile I could.

But I knew a kiss-off when I heard one.

Jett didn't seem fazed. Nor did he move to Laney's spot. He simply slid her plate in front of him. "Good thing I love chicken piccata. It's great here." He cut himself a piece.

I'd ordered the same thing, and it was delicious. I continued to eat. I wasn't really sure what else to do.

A couple of teenage girls clambered over to our table and asked Jett for an autograph. He was gracious, engaging them in a short conversation. I was impressed.

"Does that happen every time you go out?" I asked.

"Not every time, but it's a good bet."

"You were really nice to them."

"Why shouldn't I be? I'd be nothing without fans."

"Wow. That's a great attitude. I wish more celebrities shared it."

"As I just told you, sweetheart. I'm not most people."

I was beginning to see that. I really wished he would

stop the sweetheart thing though. I had nothing against endearments, but I liked for them to actually mean something.

"So tell me," he went on. "Why did you choose writing over performing? A beautiful woman like you could make a mint in this business."

"Seriously? Beautiful women are a dime a dozen here. Plus, my talent isn't in the performing arts."

"Starlets these days don't have to have talent, sweetheart."

He thought I was special, huh? His words certainly were no indication. "I suppose not. They just have to be willing to sleep their way to the top." I took my napkin off my lap and set it across my plate of half-finished food. "That's not who I am. We're done here." I stood, grabbed my messenger bag, and walked toward the entryway.

CHAPTER ELEVEN

JETT

Heather Myles was far from the first woman who had walked out on me in a huff.

She was, however, the first one I ever went after.

That fact unnerved me a bit.

I clearly knew this place better than she did. By taking a different route, I beat her to the front door of the restaurant and blocked her exit.

She stood with her hands on her hips, looking adorably obstinate. "You're in my way."

"That's right, sweetheart."

"So get out of my way."

"You haven't finished your lunch."

"Suddenly I'm no longer hungry."

I couldn't resist. "Well, it just so happens that I am. For this." I pulled her into my body and crushed my mouth to hers.

She kept her lips pressed together tightly, but I didn't give in. Restaurant customers milled around us, so I maneuvered us away from the doorway and into the coatroom, which was never used because no one ever wore a coat in LA.

I pinned her against the wall and murmured, "Open for

me, Heather. Please."

She parted her lips on a sigh, her bag dropping to the floor with a thud.

And I dived in.

She tasted as sweet as she had last night, with a little tang of lemon and capers from the piccata. Her tongue was still as velvety, her lips as sweet and soft.

And oh my God, her nipples were hard. I could actually feel them through the flimsy cotton of my wifebeater. Without thinking, I slid one hand up her waistline and cupped a breast. She gasped against my mouth, but she didn't stop me.

Good thing, because I wasn't sure I could have stopped. I gently squeezed the soft globe. She was more than a handful, even for my big hands. I found the hard knob of her nipple as we continued to kiss.

Every once in a while, I remembered we were in the coat room at the restaurant. But if she wasn't stopping me, why should I stop? My cock was throbbing, and I pushed it against her flat belly.

And still...she didn't stop me.

I kissed her harder, deeper, tasting every inch of the inside of her mouth.

She didn't stop me.

Finally, using all my willpower, I pulled back, breaking the kiss with a smack. "Heather, baby, if we don't stop this, I'm going to fuck you up against this wall."

Her lips were swollen and red from our kisses, her warm brown eyes heavy-lidded.

I waited for her to speak.

And waited.

She stayed silent, so I decided to ask for what I wanted.

"Do you want to go to my place?"

She bit her lower lip and nodded.

My dick grew even harder.

"That's a yes?"

"Yes," she said breathlessly.

I picked up her bag and grabbed her hand, leading her out of the restaurant and into my limo, which was parked nearby. "Home, Lars."

Heather didn't balk at getting into my limo.

"You want a drink?" I asked.

She shook her head. "No. I don't drink in the afternoon. And..."

"And?"

"And...I... I want to be totally aware of what I'm doing. What you're doing to me."

Damn. I wasn't sure I'd ever wanted a woman as much as I wanted her right at that moment. I pulled her into my arms and simply held her against me for a few seconds. The warmth of her body against mine felt...soothing. Yes, soothing. In a way I wasn't used to.

Soothing and turning me on at the same time.

One thing I was sure of—fucking Heather Myles was going to be unlike anything I'd ever experienced.

She laid her head on my shoulder, and I threaded my fingers through her auburn hair. She wore it down today. It was as silky as I had imagined, and I inhaled. Apples and coconut. Probably just her shampoo, but the scent aroused me. I inhaled again, letting the sweet aroma permeate every cell in my body.

God, I wanted her. Oddly, with any other woman, I'd have had her naked and on her back by now as we drove to the house. But not Heather Myles. Holding her was enough for now. And the thought of her naked in my limo? Didn't work. She was too classy for that. Already I knew I had to adjust my MO if I wanted her in my bed.

And God, I wanted her in my bed.

I'd have my fill of her today—well, for a few hours anyway, until I had to get ready for the concert.

When we arrived, I kissed the top of her head. I wasn't sure I'd ever done that to a woman before. "We're here."

She pulled away from me, her cheeks pink. She looked... reticent.

"You haven't changed your mind, have you?" I asked. *Because I think I might die a thousand deaths if you have.*

"No," she said shyly. "I haven't changed my mind."

"Then what is it?" I touched her cheek, thumbing it gently, her skin so delicate against my fingers.

"Just a few nerves, I guess."

"Heather, baby, there's nothing to be nervous about."

Lars came around and opened the door for us. I stood and helped Heather out.

"Wow!" Her eyes widened.

I did live in a pretty magnificent abode. "Come on." I took her hand.

She continued to gawk at everything, and I promised myself I'd give her a thorough tour some other time. Right now, she would only get a tour of my bedroom. I pulled her up my spiral staircase and led her down the hallway to my master suite.

Before I opened the door, though, I needed to taste her lips on mine. I cupped her cheeks in both my hands and lowered my mouth to hers. It was a slow kiss this time, not my usual, but it was what we both seemed to need. Our lips and tongues slid together in an unrushed melody.

After a few minutes of passionate necking, I stopped the kiss and gazed into her eyes. "Please don't tell me you changed your mind."

Where had that come from? I'd never asked any woman that question, and now I'd asked it twice.

But Heather was different. For some reason it was very important to me that she be all in for this.

"I haven't changed my mind, Jett."

The first time she'd used my name. Sounded wonderful coming from her lips, yet it was another name I longed to hear.

I clutched the doorknob to my room and turned it. We walked through a small sitting area and into the room and toward my bed.

Heather let out a gasp.

CHAPTER TWELVE

HEATHER

"What is it, baby?" Jett asked.

"This is your bedroom, right?"

"Of course. Why would I take you to someone else's bedroom?"

"Then it might interest you to know that there's already a woman in your bed."

I recognized her. She was the black woman from last night, the one who had put on the floorshow with a blonde. She had a smoking-hot body and an even prettier face. Naked and tangled in Jett's red silk sheets, she made me look like last night's dog food.

How had I fallen into this stupid trap? Had I been so naïve to think Jett Draconis might actually want me?

Come on, feet. Move. But I stood there, immobile, like a statue.

Jett turned. "Fuck." He headed to the bed and roused the sleeping woman. "Janet, I told you and Lindy to get out of here."

Lindy? *Two* of them had been here? Jett had obviously engaged in an interesting threesome after leaving me.

Still, my feet stayed planted.

"Lindy?" Janet said. "Where is she?"

"She's gone, like you're supposed to be," Jett said. "Get up and get dressed and get out of here."

"Hey, baby, not so fast." She sat up and looked over toward me. "I see you brought company. She's cute, though a little overdressed." She smiled at me flirtatiously and waggled her tongue. "Ever had a girl go down on you, honey? I'd love to get a taste of your hot pussy. And I know Jett here would love to watch."

That did it. "I'm so out of here." I turned toward the door.

Jett ran ahead of me, blocking me. "Please. Don't go. I thought she'd be gone by now. And nothing—"

"You *thought* she'd be gone? Plus, another one was here with her?" I shook my head. "What the hell was I thinking?"

But I knew what I had been thinking. I was thinking I wanted one romp with someone as amazingly sexy as Jett Draconis. Just one. I'd known going into this that I was one of many and nothing special to him, despite the words he'd used.

But being slapped in the face with it was a little more than I'd bargained for.

"She doesn't mean anything to me."

I turned to look at Janet, who was still sitting on the bed. Jett's words didn't seem to faze her, which made me think about the truth of the matter. Jett didn't mean anything to her, either. She just liked to fuck rock stars. She liked to fuck other women to turn rock stars on. She and Jett were two peas in a pod.

A pod I didn't belong anywhere near.

I regarded Janet. She was hot, and despite what I'd told Susie, on occasion I'd fantasized about being with a woman. I found black women particularly beautiful. I loved their skin, and they aged so gracefully.

Okay, why was that thought even in my head? This was too weird.

I wasn't going to hop into bed with Janet just to give Jett a hard-on, no matter how sexy she was. No way. That wasn't why I'd come here. At the moment, I couldn't quite remember why I had.

"Goodbye," I said, leaving the bedroom.

He followed me, grabbing my arm and turning me toward him. "Please."

One word. *Please.*

No excuses. No explanations. No promises. Just *please.*

That one word in his husky, low voice was enough to make me look into his hazel eyes. And what I saw there riveted me.

I saw warmth, sorrow, and of course, lust.

"I'm sorry," he said. "They were here last night, but I didn't—"

I placed two fingers on his full lips. "You don't owe me anything."

He seemed genuinely surprised at my reaction. "Then you'll stay?"

I had to laugh at that one. "No. I won't stay." Oh, I wanted to. What I was feeling for the man was a mass of physical lust, but something else was edging its way in. Something I had to stop dead in its tracks.

"Please," he said again.

Didn't have near the effect on me the second time around. "I knew you were no saint. No virgin. I'm not some innocent who agreed to come up here. But to go into your bedroom and find another woman already there? That's a little much for me."

"I want *you*, Heather. Not Janet. Not anyone else."

"Yes. I know. You want me. Right now. And after an hour of fucking me, you'll be done. I get that. I thought I was okay with it, but it turns out I'm not. So I'm leaving." I grabbed my phone out of my bag to contact Uber.

He pulled it from my hands. "If you're intent on leaving, Lars will drive you home."

"No, thank you." I grabbed my phone back.

Janet bustled out of the room then, as scantily dressed as she'd been at the party last night. "Ta ta," she said, blowing kisses. "So sorry we didn't get to know each other better," she added, eyeing me. She scurried down the stairs.

"See? She's gone now."

"I'm sorry," I said. "The moment has passed."

"But you wanted me, Heather. I felt it. I *still* feel it."

"You don't always get everything you want in this life." How well I knew that.

"But this is something you *can* have. I'm right here. And I want you. So much." He pulled me into his arms.

As in the limo, he didn't try to kiss me. He just held me close, our bodies touching top to bottom.

How easy it would be to melt into him, to let myself go just this once.

So he had a gorgeous woman in his bed. So he'd fucked

someone else mere hours ago. He was a rock star. What else did I expect?

Then it hit me. That was the problem. I *did* expect more. I expected more from someone who was a true artist. I'd learned a lot about Jett Draconis in the half hour we'd spent together in his limo early this morning. He was educated, intelligent, intuitive.

He was a nice man.

Nice men were hard to find in LA.

If I slept with him, let myself be intimate, I'd want more from this nice man. I'd want things he wasn't willing to give—things his current lifestyle wouldn't *allow* him to give.

I pulled away. "No. I'm sorry."

"Some other time, then?"

I shook my head.

"At least come to my concert tonight. I'll leave a front-row ticket for you at the door."

"I was there last night, remember? I've seen the show. Besides, I have to work tonight." I could easily get my shift covered, but he didn't have to know that.

"I'll make it worth your while."

I opened my mouth to respond "no" once more, but—

"*Please.*"

◆ ◆ ◆ ◆

Front row center. Strangers on each side. And as I looked up into the hazel eyes of the man who had invited me, I felt as though he were singing directly to me.

Seeing Jett perform this close was a new experience—one

I couldn't have begun to imagine.

The content of the concert was identical to the previous night. So what was different?

The way he looked at me, seemingly *only* at me.

The gentleness in his eyes when he crooned his signature ballad, "My Song is for You."

He'd written the song two years before. It had climbed the charts and was his second platinum hit after the rock classic "Heat my Blood" that had made him and Emerald Phoenix famous. He *hadn't* written the song for me. But as he sang, his eyes the color of a forest at dusk, his perfectly toned body moving in languid time with the smooth melody, his hips gyrating, his fingers making the guitar croon along with him...I almost felt as though the beautiful words beginning in those gifted vocal cords and flowing from his gorgeous full lips had been written not only about me, but *because* of me.

I stood and swayed slowly, my eyes heavy-lidded, forgetting about the strangers next to me. The concert hall was empty. Only I was in the audience, and only Jett was on stage. Only I could hear his deep voice, his beautiful words.

And only he and I were moved by them—the only two people who mattered in the world.

I floated away on a fantasy.

I lay in a cloud of cotton candy, stretched languidly, my body in zero gravity. In front of me, Jett stood, no shirt on, just his gorgeous rock-hard chest with a smattering of black hairs scattered over it.

He no longer held his vivid green electric guitar, yet the melody from his instrument still floated around us. His hair hung in soft waves around his shoulders as his full lips brought forth the words to his song.

My song is for you. You know who you are,
Heather...
Heather...
Heather...

His green-brown eyes blazed with lust. And beyond the lust, a stronger emotion burned. One I felt burning within me.

Heather... Heather... Hea—

Something jerked me from my dreamy illusion. Strong arms gripped me and pulled me onto the stage against a granite-like chest. I looked up into the wide eyes of Jett Draconis.

"What are you doing? What's going on?"

He didn't respond.

The crowd became chaotic, and two armed guards ran toward Jett, forcing him backstage.

Words came over the loudspeaker in the concert hall, but they were jumbled and made no sense to me.

My whole reality was being in Jett's arms, being whisked away. Where? I didn't know, and at this moment I didn't care. My mind told me I should be scared, but with Jett's strong arms protecting me, I couldn't bring that emotion to the surface. I shuddered, yes, but was it from fear? No. It was from being close to Jett again, from the energy of his music, from the wildness and chaos of the converging crowd of people.

I was safe. I had no doubt. Whatever was going on....Jett would keep me safe.

Something had happened. That much was clear. But no one was telling me anything.

"Leave the girl," one of the guards said.

Jett pushed the guard away and continued forward. A moment later we were safely ensconced in his limo.

Noise echoed around us and fans knocked on the windows, demanding to know what was going on. The limousine lurched. Stopped. Then lurched again.

"What's going on, Lars?" Jett said into his intercom.

"Sorry, sir. They're all around us. I can't move without hitting someone."

"Don't harm anyone. Let the guards take care of it. We're safe in here." Then he looked at me, his eyes ablaze. "*You're* safe in here. With me."

"Why did you—"

He silenced me with a kiss. A firm, sedating kiss, and I surrendered to the moment, letting my tongue duel with his. What had happened didn't matter anymore. All that mattered was that I was here, with Jett, safe in his limo. Safe in his arms. His lips on mine.

The kiss broke when the limousine lurched again, forcing us apart.

"God, Heather," he said. "All I could think about was getting to you."

"What happened? Why did you jump down and pull me onstage?"

"Someone called in a bomb threat."

I gasped.

"We got a message in our headsets while we were on stage to stop playing and exit out the rear of the concert hall. Didn't you see the rest of them leave?"

I couldn't tell him that I had been in the midst of a fantasy about him singing only to me when this all occurred. "No," I said shakily.

"Didn't you hear the announcement over the speakers? When the crowd went nuts?"

"N-No." I'd been too engrossed in my fantasy, and then, when Jett grabbed me, I hadn't been able to think at all.

"This happened once before, at a concert in Philadelphia a year ago. I didn't waste any time getting off stage that time. This time..."

"Yeah?" I said, still shivering.

"This time..." His silk hair drifted over his shoulders. "This time I couldn't leave. Not without you."

CHAPTER THIRTEEN

JETT

I reached out to touch her soft cheek, and the limo lurched again, forcing my hand onto her breast. I removed it quickly. "I'm sorry."

"It's okay," she said.

My heart was beating so quickly. Something was percolating in me, something I had never experienced. Unlike the last time this had happened, when my first thought had been to save my own ass, this time was different.

I had placed Heather at the concert, in the front row. If anything had happened to her...

It would've been my fault.

I felt responsible. Nothing more. Still, as she sat next to me in my limo, each lurch bringing her closer to me, I couldn't shake the feeling of need that was consuming me.

Lars would take us to my place. Heather hadn't said anything. Was she expecting me to take her home first? I'd had a chance with her this afternoon, but Janet had blown it for me. I couldn't blame Heather for not believing that I hadn't touched either of those women last night, even though it was true. Tonight there would be no after-party. The hall would be cleared out and searched by the bomb squad.

No Janet. No Lindy. No groupies. And no bandmates like Zane trying to coerce me into partying harder. No drugs and alcohol flowing.

Tonight...only the beautiful woman next to me.

Surely once I had fucked her, the strange compulsion to have her would dissipate.

Surely...

I couldn't allow myself to think otherwise. Lars had finally gotten the limo moving, and I knew where we were headed. While I wanted to remain silent, words edged out of my throat.

"Baby, we're going to my place. Tell me now if you want me to take you home first."

"I..."

"Yeah?"

"I...don't know what I want, to be honest. This afternoon, I wanted you so much."

"I wanted you too, Heather. I still want you."

"I feel so..." She rubbed her upper arms as a shudder rocked her body.

"Don't be scared, baby."

"I didn't know what was happening."

"I should've explained. I'm sorry I didn't. I just had to get you out of there. That was the only thought on the surface of my mind. 'Get Heather out. Keep Heather safe.'"

She gave me a weak smile. "Thank you for that. I've heard of things like this. Of people panicking and causing a stampede. People getting trampled..."

"That wasn't going to happen to you on my watch."

"What about the others? Thank God Susie didn't go to the concert tonight."

"The guards and the cops will take care of the others. There were no casualties in Philly. I have only the best people working for me."

I hoped I wasn't feeding her a load of bullshit. There hadn't been any casualties the last time, but I had no idea what was going on right now. All I knew was I had to protect Heather. Not just from a bomb or stampede, but from any bad thoughts entering her head.

Emotion coiled through me—new emotion I'd never felt before.

Part of it made me want to squirm, stop the car, and get out and run until it went away.

But another part of it...calmed me. Offered me peace.

That part kept me grounded, kept the desire to protect the woman next to me close to my heart.

"I'm glad," Heather said. "I know you would feel terrible if anything happened to your fans."

Her attitude shocked me, but only for a moment. Heather was concerned not for herself, not even for me, but for the throngs of people who had been in the concert hall.

"I've never met anyone like you before," I said. And I wasn't sure I'd ever uttered a truer statement in my life.

That got a cute little chuckle out of her. "I'm nothing special."

"Baby, all I know is that I was willing to throw myself into a burning fire to get you out of there safely tonight. That has never happened to me."

Her red lips curved into a beautiful smile. "Thank you again."

"You don't have to keep thanking me. That's not why I told you that."

"Then why did you tell me? To try to get me into your bed again?"

A spark of emotion coursed through me. Not anger. Not sadness. Perhaps just a little disappointment. Because although I did want to bed her—I could never deny that—the prospect of fucking her tight little body hadn't entered my mind when I risked my life to save hers.

So why had I done it?

Truthfully, I wasn't sure.

"No, Heather. I told you. Tell me if you want me to take you home, and I will."

She touched my cheek this time, her fingertips burning a silky trail on my flesh, and gazed into my eyes. "No, Jett. I don't want you to take me home." She pulled my face toward her and gave me a soft kiss on the tip of my nose.

No woman had ever kissed me there before, and it was.... endearing. And a turn-on. Of course, everything about Heather Myles turned me on.

I took her lips in a searing kiss, and we made out like a couple of teenagers until we got to my mansion.

When Lars opened the door for us and helped Heather out, I followed, grabbed her hand, and we practically ran into the house and up the spiral staircase to my bedroom.

I flattened her against my bedroom door and kissed her again, wet and openmouthed, devouring her. Her breasts swelled, and her nipples tightened against my chest. She had worn a light-pink tank top, no bra—God, help me—to the concert.

Because of the lighting, I hadn't been able to see her while I was on stage, but I knew where her seat was, and I directed all my passion, all my energy toward that seat. If I'd been able to see those hard nipples poking out through her top, I wouldn't have been able to perform.

But I was able to perform now—a performance of a different nature.

She was so fucking beautiful. So fucking hot.

My cock was thick and hard against her tummy, and when she reached down and grabbed it, I nearly spilled.

I quickly opened the door to my bedroom, hauled her inside, and shut it behind us. To my surprise, she dropped to her knees, unsnapped my jeans, and pushed them over my hips. My cock sprang out, ready and willing.

She stared at me for a few seconds.

"What is it, baby?" I didn't add, "Too big for you?" With a groupie, I would have. They loved that stuff. But Heather Myles was different. I didn't want to treat her like a groupie. Or like anyone else, either. She was special.

"It's just... You're beautiful," she said.

A shudder surged through my body. Her words... They made me feel things. Things foreign to me.

I liked the feelings. They weren't anything I could keep. I knew that. But for tonight, I would let myself feel these new things. These wonderful things.

Suck my cock, sweetheart. Normally that would be my

demand about now. But again, I couldn't force those words past my lips. Heather was different. So I chose different words.

"Please, Heather. Please put your mouth on me."

Her big brown eyes went wide, and she backed away. "I'm sorry. I'm not usually so forward."

"I don't have any issues with you being forward, baby."

"It's just... You've been with so many women. And I'm afraid..."

"You'd pale in comparison?" I said, chuckling.

"God! No!" She backed off even farther, sitting down on the floor with a plunk.

I wished I could take my stupid words back. Heather was being sensible. She wasn't worried she couldn't pass muster. She wanted to make sure I was clean before she put my cock in her mouth. I only respected her more for it.

"Baby, I'm sorry. I was being a dick. I want you. I told you in the limo that you were safe with me, and I meant it. I'm clean. I always use condoms, and I get tested once every three months."

Her cheeks turned rosy.

"It's a valid concern, Heather. I understand."

She sat for a few seconds longer, and then, to my astonishment, she rose to her knees and planted a kiss right on the head of my cock.

I let out a low moan. That one touch of her lips to my most sensitive flesh excited me more than the best blowjob Lindy and Janet had ever given me in tandem.

She kissed my flesh again, and then trailed tiny kisses all the way up my shaft to my balls. She inhaled and then planted the same little kisses as my sack tightened. Then she licked my shaft with one long stroke of her warm velvety tongue, bringing her back to my cockhead.

"God, baby."

She sucked my tip, making me crazy. And when I thought I couldn't stand the suspense any longer, she took me about three-quarters of the way into her mouth.

Damn. Hold it. I clenched my teeth. *Not going to come yet. Not going to ruin this night.*

I hadn't yet touched her bare breasts. I hadn't sucked on those beautiful little nipples. I hadn't looked at her pussy, tasted her sweet cream.

I closed my eyes. She pulled back and then sucked me even farther into her sweet mouth.

Oh, God... My balls crunched close to my body, and the tiny convulsions began.

No stopping it now.

I was coming—coming in her beautiful mouth.

I hoped she wouldn't mind... Hoped—

"Ah, God!" The moan echoed throughout the room as I spurted down her throat.

She didn't bat an eye. She took me, took all of me, seeming to savor every drop as I coated her mouth and throat.

The orgasm surged through me, along with ecstasy I had never known. As my cock pulsated, so did every cell of my body, so did my thundering heart.

When I finally stopped convulsing, she moved backward a bit, my cock, still hard, falling from her mouth. She licked her full red lips, but still a drop of my come drizzled down her chin.

She had never looked more beautiful.

But she would. After I had thoroughly fucked her, she would be even more beautiful, lying naked amidst my satin sheets, her limbs tangled within them, her nipples ruddy and puffy from being sucked and kissed, her pussy swollen and sated, pink and glistening.

Yes, she would be even more beautiful.

And now that I had come already? I could take the time to worship her body the way she deserved.

CHAPTER FOURTEEN

HEATHER

I wasn't sure what had gotten into me. I had plenty of sexual experience, but it wasn't like me to be so forward. Then, after he'd assured me it was safe, I had simply followed my instincts, my intuition, had let my body take over and do what it wanted to do.

And it had wanted to kneel before Jett Draconis and suck his magnificent cock.

It was a surprise to me. I didn't mind giving head, but it had never been my favorite thing to do during sex. Something inside me had taken over. I had wanted Jett's cock in my mouth. I had wanted to please him. I had been compelled to kneel in front of him.

I had never swallowed before. I had never imagined wanting to.

But when I had felt Jett start to come, desire had flooded my mind. Desire had flooded *me*. Desire to taste him, to taste every part of him, to swallow whatever he chose to give me.

It had been the most intimate experience of my life.

And I wanted more.

He had softened a little after he had come, but as I gazed

at him now, he was hardening.

Good, because I truly hoped we weren't done.

"Heather," he said, his voice husky.

"Yeah?"

"I'm sorry I didn't warn you. Didn't give you a choice..."

I smiled. "It's okay. I...enjoyed it."

"Thank God," he said, his voice low and husky. "Now, stand up."

I obeyed, and he pulled the cotton tank over my head. I lifted my arms to help, and soon it was strewn over a chair.

He cupped my breasts. "As gorgeous as I remember."

From when he'd caught me masturbating. But I wasn't embarrassed, not even slightly. I sighed as he lightly stroked my nipples. They strained forward, and I yearned for his lips on them. But he went slowly, so achingly slowly. He skimmed his fingers and palms over the indentation of my waist, over my abdomen, and then up my arms and shoulders to my neck. He cupped my cheeks.

"You're so beautiful," he said. "You actually glow, Heather. As if there's a fiery opal inside you, illuminating you. You're dazzling."

My mouth dropped open, but I didn't know why I was surprised. The man was an artist. Not just a musician but a poet. He wrote most of his own lyrics.

Suddenly, the most important thing in my world became lighting up for him, giving him everything inside me that I could possibly give. Would I get the same in return?

Didn't matter.

This was for me. Not for him or anyone else. This was *my*

choice, and I was prepared to live with the consequences.

Come on, Heather. You're hoping he'll fall in love with you.

Perhaps part of me was, but my rational mind knew better. Jett Draconis was a rock star, a celebrity of mega proportions. I was a failing screenwriter who was pretty and had a nice body, but I couldn't compete in a beauty contest with the woman I'd found in his bed earlier.

I had to be okay with that.

I was.

Or at least I'd try to be.

One thing was certain—I wasn't missing this opportunity. Something in Jett Draconis called to me, made me want to give everything. Things I'd never given before.

No man had ever had such an effect on me.

I feared no man ever would again.

But I banished that fear from my head. Today, I would let my body take the lead.

Jett lowered his head and kissed one of my nipples. I nearly shattered at the wild sensation. Not just his full, firm lips on my sensitive flesh, but his long hair tickling my shoulders and upper breasts.

Long hair on a man was so sexy. But hell, Jett would be sexy without any hair at all.

He trailed those long, thick fingers down my arms to my waistline and began working on my jeans. I was already wet. I could feel it. His warm hands on my flesh made me tingle all over. He was still kissing my nipple, going slowly. I had to bite my lip to keep from yelling at him to take it between his lips. To chew on it.

Once he got my jeans unzipped, he thrust his hand inside my panties.

Then he did suck on my nipple, but when I felt his fingers glide through my folds, he dropped the nipple with a soft pop.

"My God, you're soaked." He breathed against my flesh. "Fuck, baby."

I let out a slow moan. Images conjured in my head of the two of us joined together on his bed. How I wanted him. Then his fingers grazed my clit.

I nearly imploded on the spot.

I wanted his hands everywhere, his mouth everywhere, tantalizing me, torturing me. Too many clothes. My tank was gone, but my jeans were still around my hips. I pulled away, though removing his fingers from my pussy was pure torture.

I flipped off my sandals and shimmied out of my jeans and panties until I stood before him, naked as the day I was born.

His hazel eyes were wide and smoldering. His jeans were pulled down to his thighs, but other than that he was still fully clothed.

I took his hand. "Please. Just take me to your bed."

He yanked up his pants without snapping them, lifted me in his arms, and walked through the sitting area over to his bed. Thankfully it had been made, and the sheets were different from the ones I had seen earlier with another woman's limbs tangled in them.

He set me down gently, more gently than I had expected, and then gazed at me.

My body flushed with warmth. I looked down, and the top of my breasts were rosy pink. My nipples stood straight out, ready and willing, wanting more of his lips, his tongue, his teeth. Everything. I wanted everything this man could give me. For once, I would know what it felt like to be worshiped by a man who was as beautiful as a god.

Slowly he began to undress. First he took off his black boots—motorcycle boots that he had been wearing on stage. Then he unbuttoned his jeans, also black. The men of Emerald Phoenix never wore the tight clothes many other rockers wore. They wore boots, jeans, and either tank tops or T-shirts. And they were all the sexier for it.

Jett wore a black T-shirt, no logo. When he'd disposed of his boots, he pulled the shirt over his head.

God, his chest. Just the right amount of hair to make him masculine but not furry. Perfectly formed reddish nipples, already erect, a six pack, and that beautiful V that led to the wonderful cock I'd already seen...and would see again in mere seconds.

He pushed his black jeans and boxers over what turned out to be perfectly muscled hips and thighs. Soon those garments joined his boots and T-shirt on the floor.

My mouth dropped open.

As beautiful as Jett was fully clothed, naked he was... What was the word he'd used for me?

Dazzling.

Jett Draconis was dazzling.

He threaded his fingers through his long hair, whisking it out of his eyes. "Let me look at you, Heather. I just want to look at you. Take in your beauty."

I couldn't help a sigh. It escaped my lips before I even

knew it. My nipples strained forward, aching for him.

"Please, Jett."

"I will. I'll give you everything you want. In a minute. But I haven't had my fill of just looking at you yet."

Was he like this with every woman he bedded? Most likely these were all lines, tried-and-true, that he had used many times before.

The thing of it was? I didn't care. It didn't matter to me in this moment whether he had used those lines a thousand times before. Because the way he looked at me, the low rasp of his voice, the way his huge cock was straining forward, I could imagine he was uttering those words for the very first time.

My arousal wafted toward me, that scent of apples and musk. The smell of my sex.

Finally, Jett lowered himself onto the bed. He held himself above me, our lips mere inches apart. I closed my eyes, waiting for his kiss.

His kiss never came.

At least not to my mouth.

Moist lips clamped around my clit, and his rough tongue scorched across my pussy folds.

I lifted my hips, straining for more.

But Jett Draconis was a tease. He licked my clit, licked my pussy lips, delved even lower and licked the crease of my ass. He went back and forth to each spot, and just as I was getting really turned on, he left and teased me somewhere else.

"My God," I moaned. "Please."

With that, he sucked my labia into his mouth and tugged. I thrashed my head to each side, lifting my hips farther. Then his lips clamped around my swollen clit, and he sucked.

I was on the edge, tingles racing across my skin, diving inside me, and hurling themselves toward my core.

When he thrust one of his thick fingers inside me...I shattered.

The orgasm was quick and catapulted me into oblivion. I moaned, saying his name over and over. "Jett. Jett. Jett."

"That's it, baby. Let me make you feel good."

My slick channel stretched, and I realized he had added another one of his long, thick fingers. I closed my eyes, reveling in the feelings he was evoking in my body.

"You smell so good, baby. You taste so good. So fucking sweet." He licked my clit some more, sucking it, tugging on it, and I flew into another climax.

I grasped at his bedsheets, my fists full of the silky fabric.

From somewhere, his deep voice echoed, "Got to have you. Need to be inside you."

A rip of a condom wrapper. Then—

I was full, so full. His cock filling up every empty place in my body that I had ever known.

I hadn't known I felt so empty until he filled me.

A deep, low, long groan emerged from his throat. And then my name.

"Heather. God, Heather."

Not sweetheart. Not baby.

Heather.

I opened my eyes and gazed into his. They had darkened into a nutty brown, and they looked into mine with something I hadn't seen before.

Lust was there, yes. But so was something else.

Almost like... reverence.

"Heather. My God. It feels so good to be inside you."

I opened my mouth to return his words, but all that came out was a soft sigh.

I wanted to tell him how much he was filling the emptiness in my soul, emptiness I never knew was there. I knew this was a one-time thing, and I couldn't say those words.

But I could show him. I grasped his head, sinking my fingers into his gorgeous locks, and pulled him toward me until his lips touched mine. The kiss was electric this time, and the taste of my own musk on his tongue made it even more so. I ravished his mouth and dueled with his tongue as our lips slid against each other's in a kiss that rocked my world.

All the while he plunged in and out of me, his cock stretching me in exquisite pleasure. To be so full, so full of everything that had once been lacking in my life...

He ripped his mouth away and inhaled. "God, baby. Your kisses. Your pussy. Everything about you." And then he crushed his lips to mine once more.

Another spark-filled kiss. I couldn't get enough of his tongue, of his lips, of his cock thrusting into me, filling me.

If only it wouldn't end...

But when he thrust into me one last time with a growl, I knew he had emptied himself into me.

We lay there for a moment, still joined.

And for one instant, I wished we could stay that way forever.

CHAPTER FIFTEEN

JETT

Effort. I needed effort to pull my lips away from hers, to pull my cock out of her sweet, succulent pussy.

I wanted to stay embedded inside her, her walls hugging me, her sweet lips sliding over mine.

I ground into her mouth once more and then broke the kiss. I rolled over, letting my cock slide out of her warmth. I quickly left the bed and disposed of the soiled condom.

When I returned, I simply regarded her. Oddly, I couldn't seem to get enough of looking at her. And now, against my mahogany sheets, her body full and flushed and looking so thoroughly used, I feared I might never be able to tear my eyes away from her.

She smiled and closed her eyes, a silky sigh escaping her throat. I walked toward my window and looked out at the LA night.

But for that bomb threat, we would be at the after-party right now.

Of course, I hadn't intended to stay at the party very long. My plan had been to get Heather to come home with me.

God bless the bomb threat.

I sincerely hoped no one had been injured while fleeing the concert hall. I didn't want that on my head. But the thought was fleeting. Especially when I turned back around and took a look at the beauty that lay tangled within my linens.

She was covered in a sheen of light perspiration, her reddish-brown hair matted against her forehead and sticking to her shoulders and neck. Her eyes were closed now, her dark brown lashes a velvety curtain against her skin. Her lips were red and swollen from our passionate kisses, her breasts rosy, and the paradise between her legs dark pink and engorged.

Beautiful. So fucking beautiful.

Her body was long and lean, her breasts the perfect size. Her hips swelled just the right amount, and her legs were shapely and had wrapped around me perfectly as I pumped in and out of her.

Then I noticed her breathing. Regular, with a soft snore every couple of breaths. I chuckled. Adorable. Everything about her was wonderful, even the little snore.

I longed to wake her up, to shove my cock into her again and again, to spend more time on those beautiful nipples, to kiss every inch of flesh on her body.

But something else niggled at me, something I longed for even more than taking her again.

To snuggle up next to her, to sleep with her. To wake up in the morning with her beside me.

I had never had such a thought, and it frightened me. We hardly knew each other, but what I did know I liked. She was educated, serious about her craft. I loved the music I made, but I missed opera, and I sometimes wondered if I'd made the right choice to pursue a different type of music. Of course I'd had no guarantees I would become a rock icon. And no doubt I'd had a lot of help along the way.

Help I didn't want to think about right now.

Classical music filled the air. The overture from *The Marriage of Figaro*. My ring tone. I rushed to find my discarded jeans on the floor and grabbed my cell phone before it woke Heather.

I recognized the number.

And I knew better than to ignore the call.

Still naked, I walked into my bathroom and shut the door.

"Yeah?" I said into the phone.

"Did you have fun with your little whore tonight?"

"I don't think that's any of your business."

"We had a deal. You can fuck as many groupies as you want, but you don't get attached."

"Look, Alicia. I don't have time for this right now."

"Oh? Need to get back to your little slut?"

"She's not a slut, damn it."

"I was right. You have feelings for this one. Why else would you have rescued her in the middle of a bomb threat?"

"Having me followed again?"

"I don't have to have you followed. You're headline news. The paparazzi had a field day with this one. Everyone is wondering who the girl is that you risked your life to carry out of the concert during a bomb threat."

Of course everyone was wondering. I couldn't make a move without the world knowing. This life was getting old quickly.

"It's the middle of the night!"

"This city never sleeps. Just remember who made all this happen for you...and who can take it all away just as fast." The line went dead.

Alicia Hopkins.

My benefactor. A billionaire heiress who had propelled me to the top faster than I would've ever been able to get there on my own. I had let myself become her pet project. And along the way, I had given her everything else she wanted from me.

We'd had a brief affair, but when I made it to the top, my publicist said I was a commodity. I had to be available, single. Being seen on the arm of a woman twenty years my senior wouldn't be good for the rock star image.

But by then, Alicia had become obsessed.

So I had made a deal with the devil. I could have the life she'd made for me, but no matter who I slept with, I was hers. Only hers. Why? I didn't want to think about the reason when a gorgeous woman was in my bed.

I opened the door and left the bathroom. Heather lay in the same place I'd left her, still snoring softly.

In the morning, I would no doubt feel better about everything. I could fuck her once more before she left, and that would probably get her out of my system. After all, it had worked before with other women.

The problem was Heather Myles wasn't just any woman.

And if I was honest with myself, I had known that when I first laid eyes on her.

I sighed. Heather was a nice girl, someone who didn't deserve to be thrown into the craziness that had become my life.

I got into bed and lay down next to her. If only she didn't fit so perfectly against my body. If only she hadn't curled into me in her sleep.

If only...

I closed my eyes. But sleep didn't come for hours.

I awoke to Heather's lips around my cock. I was hard, of course. I was usually hard in the morning, and my dick hadn't gone down at all since I'd been in Heather's presence. Except for when I'd been talking to Alicia on the phone. That was always a boner killer.

It wasn't the best blowjob I'd ever had. She couldn't take me quite as far as Janet or suck quite as hard as Lindy. But my God, the feelings she evoked within me.

I was ready to come in her mouth, but I needed to be inside that sweet heaven.

"Come here, baby. Sit on me."

She smiled shyly, crawled forward, and positioned herself above my cock.

"Wait, baby... The condom..."

"I'm on the pill. And I haven't been with anyone in a while. I'm clean, Jett."

The feel of her silky walls against mine, with no barrier... It would be heaven. "God, Heather, what are you doing to me?"

She sank down upon my cock. "What you asked. Riding you. Fucking you."

But that wasn't what I had meant. She had gotten inside

me somehow. Stirred up emotions I had left dormant far too long. Emotions that would eventually be my undoing.

I couldn't put her through that.

As much as it pained me, I grabbed her hips and lifted her off my cock.

CHAPTER SIXTEEN

HEATHER

Had I done something wrong?

My body reacted, the desire still pulsating through me. On the edge. Needed satisfaction. Was willing to do almost anything. So close. Just one more millimeter to the precipice...

But I had been yanked off his cock. Yanked off the instrument giving me so much pleasure.

"I can't do this right now," Jett said, his eyes closed.

My mouth dropped open. Wasn't he the one who had begged me to get on top of him just minutes ago?

I was a big girl. I had known what I was getting into, and I had chosen to go forward anyway.

Still... In the back of my mind, a fantasy motion picture had been playing. A fantasy that I could be the one to make Jett give up his groupies and fall in love. That I would be the one who captured his heart. In fact, I was much more disappointed than I thought I would be. Somehow, that fantasy had edged its way into my reality.

I wanted it. Longed for it.

Not that I would let him know any of that.

"Sure. I understand. No biggie." I rolled off the bed,

scanning the room for my clothes.

"Hey," he said. "Come back here for a minute."

Was he kidding? "It's okay. I get it. You're done with me."

"No, you *don't* get it. Last night... It meant something to me."

It had meant something to me too. Something amazing. But I wasn't about to admit that at the moment. "Hey, it was a fuck. It is what it is. On to the next one, right?"

He sighed and closed his eyes but then opened them again almost immediately. "Yeah. Whatever, babe."

I scurried around, grabbing clothes as quickly as I could, and then charged into the bathroom.

I couldn't stop the tears. I turned on the shower so he wouldn't hear me and then sat with a *plunk* down on the plush toilet seat.

How had I thought I could be okay?

It is what it is.

Objectively, I had expected nothing different. That was how I needed to continue to look at this—no fantasies, no feelings. Clearly that was how Jett saw it. Plus, thanks to him, a television producer was looking at my work. So television wasn't my first love. So what? Rock and roll wasn't Jett's first love either, but he was great at it, and he was still singing. Still practicing his vocation.

But I really didn't want to think about him right now. I sniffled, swallowing back the remainder of my tears. The shower was on. Why not take advantage of it? Clearly he wanted me to leave, but I had at least earned the right to a shower.

The hot water would redden my skin and help hide the fact that I'd been sobbing like an idiot. I stepped into the marble-encased shower. Pure decadence. I hadn't bothered turning on steam, but the water fell from not one but three massive showerheads. I looked around and found some shampoo and a bar of soap, but then just stood for a few moments, letting the anguish envelop me.

And then a body—a warm, wet body against mine.

"Hey," he said against my ear.

I turned into him. "For real?" I sniffled, hoping the water was hiding the tears. "You kick me out of your bed, and now you get in the shower with me?"

He pulled me into him and kissed the top of my head in an almost father-like manner. His dick, hard as ever, pressed into my belly. Not so father-like after all.

"Heather, I'm sorry."

I cleared my throat. "You have no reason to be sorry. You're done with me. I get that. I knew who you were going into this. Maybe I'm more of a groupie than I thought. Maybe I just wanted to fuck a rock star."

He shook his head. "I don't believe that. You're different."

"I'm not. I got what I came for, Jett. I hope I didn't disappoint you." Then I wanted to smack myself for saying those words. Of course I had disappointed him. I didn't have near the experience his groupies had. I opened my mouth to take back the words but then realized that would only draw more attention to them.

He pulled me close to him again. "Please, Heather. Please just let me hold you for a few more minutes."

Was he kidding?

I pulled back, nearly slipping, but he grabbed my forearm, steadying me.

"I suppose it was a little presumptuous of me to think I could use your shower."

"Damn it, it wasn't presumptuous at all. Please, come into my arms for a few minutes."

Dear God, I had no strength. As much as I wanted to stay away from him, to begin the healing of my heart, my body moved of its own accord, and I melted into his arms, my slick skin sliding against his. He felt so good against me. If only he hadn't shared with me some of the intimate details of his life—his love of opera, his true artistry. Maybe if he was *just* a guy who looked good gyrating on stage, this wouldn't hurt so damned much.

He kissed the top of my head again and rubbed my back, which was strangely soothing even as my heart was breaking. I hoped these few moments would last forever. Of course I knew better. But still they would be etched in my brain for all time. And more importantly, etched in my heart.

I waited for him to pull back, to stop the embrace. Moment by moment, however, he held me, the water still pelting us. In my apartment, the hot water would've run out by now, but he clearly had a gigantic hot water heater in this mansion.

His erection pulsed against my belly, and I ached to fall to my knees and take him into my mouth. I wanted to please him, wanted to do whatever I could to stretch out this time with him.

Still he didn't move.

So *I* would. I had to find the strength within me to leave this man I'd inadvertently fallen in love with.

How had I let this happen? I'd been serious. I'd been willing to have one night with him and then move on.

At least...I thought I had.

Turned out I wasn't that strong. But at that moment I called on that strength from the depths of my bones.

And I pulled away.

"I need to leave."

"No. Let me wash you. Let me wash your hair for you."

What a thought! Those thick fingers massaging my scalp. Then, when I turned toward the water to rinse, he could slide that magnificent cock into me from behind...

"No," I said. "I need to leave. Now." I pushed past him and stepped out of the shower, looking for something to dry off with.

He stepped out behind me and handed me a plush black bath towel. He said nothing.

I dried off quickly and began to put on my clothes.

He stood there, making no move to grant me privacy. I would have liked some, but it was his bathroom, his house. I was the stranger here, not him.

I turned around to avoid his stare and put on my panties.

His inhale was swift. "You're so beautiful, Heather."

I closed my eyes for a few seconds, breathed in, and then opened them and continued getting dressed. Then I turned, walked past him—he was still naked and erect—left the bathroom, and found my sandals. I put them on hastily and walked out of the bedroom.

"Wait!" He clambered behind me, now clad in a green silk robe. Which of course brought out the green in his eyes.

How had this happened to me?

"Let me drive you."

"No. I'll get an Uber. I'm good, but thanks." I headed down his spiral staircase.

He followed. "Please. At least let Lars drive you."

"No, thank you."

"Heather..."

I turned abruptly, nearly crashing into him. "Jett, stop it. Please. This is over. Let me go."

I turned around, headed down the rest of the staircase, through the ornate foyer, and then out the door.

Susie pounced on me when I finally made it home. I so wasn't in the mood.

"Oh my God! Lindy called me and told me Jett grabbed you after the bomb threat. Are you okay? What happened? How was it? You have to tell me everything."

Normally I would have, but I couldn't bring myself to describe my amazing—and then devastating—time in detail. Not even for one of my best friends.

"I'm fine," I said, "and nothing happened."

"You're lying. Your cheeks are red. You went off with Jett Draconis last night and you expect me to believe nothing happened? I know you too well. Or rather, I know Jett too well." She giggled.

Though I had believed Susie when she said she had never

slept with Jett, I had no doubt she knew what he was about. She had probably witnessed him in many compromising situations.

No way would she believe nothing had happened between Jett and me. So how could I get away with this without talking?

And then my phone rang. Perfect! A diversion.

"I bet that's you know who!" Susie arched her eyebrows.

We hadn't exchanged phone numbers, though my heart sped at the possibility. He could easily get my number, with all his resources. In fact, he had done so already, to give it to Laney. I glanced down at my phone. My heart surged again. It wasn't a number I recognized.

"I have to take this," I said, forcing a smile.

CHAPTER SEVENTEEN

JETT

I hadn't had my fill of Heather Myles just yet. Usually a good romp with a woman was all it took to get me to stop thinking about her. Not this time.

I'd wanted to run right after her. In fact, it had taken every bit of strength I possessed not to grab her and drag her back up to my bedroom.

I had to forget her. I couldn't pull someone as sweet and innocent as Heather into my fucked-up world.

The call from Alicia had spooked me. She didn't usually keep such close tabs on me. Of course, I hadn't ever jumped offstage to save a fan in the front row of one of my concerts from a bomb threat before.

At the time, I didn't even know why I was doing it. I had acted on pure instinct—a drive to grab Heather and get her to safety, no matter the cost. I'd certainly had my fill of women over the past five years, and every once in a while, Alicia would surface to remind me of our bargain. Never before had I worried much about it. Even though I had begun to grow bored with groupies and fans who just wanted to fuck a rock star, I never imagined I would find someone who might make me wish I hadn't made the deal.

I didn't think Heather could be that person. Not at first.

But she had spooked Alicia. Alicia had noticed something different.

And something *was* different.

I never worried about falling in love. Why would I want that when I could have a new woman each night?

I was playing around on my guitar, waiting for the rest of the band for rehearsal, when Zane walked in. Actually Zeb. Zane Michaels was the name Alicia had given my classical pianist friend Zebulon Frankfurter. Yes, that was truly his given name. She had reinvented Zeb Frankfurter from classical pianist to rock star keyboardist Zane Michaels.

She had done the same thing for Jeremy Gustafson.

Jeremy Gustafson was a classically trained bass-baritone opera vocalist.

Jeremy Gustafson was me.

The world saw Jett Draconis, but inside I was still Jeremy.

And Jeremy had fallen in love.

Unfortunately, Jeremy didn't exist anymore. Not in the real world. On the outside, I was Jett Draconis, and I wasn't allowed to fall in love. Even if I did, I could never act on it. No woman in her right mind would agree to the terms of the deal I'd made. And if I reneged on the deal?

I couldn't think about those consequences.

Maybe I was mistaken. Maybe this *wasn't* love. Maybe it was just more of a loss than I'd ever experienced. Maybe I just needed a couple more fucks of Heather Myles's tight little body to get her out of my system.

But that wouldn't happen. Heather wasn't like most women. I had essentially kicked her out of my bed this morning, and no way would she come running back. She was better than that. A class act.

"Hey, J." Zane sauntered by me to his keyboard. "Where are the other guys?"

I fiddled with a few more chords. "Don't know. I'm sure they'll be here in a few."

"Have you heard anything new about the bomb threat last night?" Zane asked.

I shook my head. "Nope. Probably just a hoax, like most of them are."

"Yeah. At least no one was hurt." Zane sat down at his keyboard, flipping some buttons. "I had an amazing time last night. Four women at once, man. We sure as hell weren't getting laid like this when we were doing the classical shit."

Four women at once. I'd had four women at once. Hell, Zane and I had had four women together. We'd done the group thing, the orgy thing, everything. Zane obviously hadn't had his fill yet.

"Do you ever regret it?" I asked.

"Regret what?"

"Letting Alicia take us to the top?"

"Nope. This is the life, man. More money and more women than we ever thought possible. What's to regret?"

"We're not doing what we set out to do."

"Man, I'm playing piano. So it's a great big electric number and not a nine-foot Steinway. I can live with that. You're singing. You're a fucking sensation, J. You live in a mansion.

You have everything you could possibly want."

I couldn't fault his words. Except that there were some things money couldn't buy.

I'd made a deal to get to the top.

And I had regrets.

"So how'd it go with you last night?" Zane asked. "Did you get inside that cute little redhead's pants?"

Normally I would've said yes. But Heather wasn't a woman that men talked about. I didn't want to talk about her in that way, not even with my best friend.

So I shook my head. "Turns out she's not interested."

"Not interested how? Or maybe *you* were the one who ended up not being interested."

I could easily agree. Could easily say she wasn't my thing. She was bad in bed. Yada yada yada. But it would be a big fat lie.

I owed Heather more than that.

"I was surprised too. But I guess rock stars just aren't her thing."

"Sorry, dude. If I'd known you went home alone..."

"What? You would've given up one of your four women for me?" I laughed. "Good one, Z."

"Yeah." He laughed as well. "I was wondering if you would buy that one."

Tony and the rest of the guys arrived, the techs did our sound check, and we started our rehearsal.

But my heart wasn't in it.

The fact wasn't lost on the guys. When we took our first break, Tony said, "What's up with you, J? Something bothering you today?"

"No, I'm good."

"You're not in the game. Where's your brain?"

"I think it's with a cute little redhead," Zane said. "A cute little redhead who apparently doesn't dig rock stars."

"I'm cool, guys. There's no redhead."

"You jumped off stage for her," Tony said. "It's going to be all over the tabloids today. You do know that, don't you?"

I sighed. Yes, I did know that. Heather didn't deserve any of this. She didn't deserve any of the fallout it would create. So it was better for the world to think she had turned me down. I could take it. There were ten women at any time who wanted to be in my bed.

I couldn't pursue Heather Myles. I couldn't fall in love.

The only answer was to never see her again.

CHAPTER EIGHTEEN

HEATHER

I put my phone to my ear. "Hello?"

"Is this Heather Myles?" a female voice said.

My heart fell. My head had known Jett wouldn't be calling me. My heart, however, had been hoping. Just like that, my hopes were dashed.

"Yes, this is Heather."

"Hi there, Heather. My name is Alicia Hopkins."

Alicia Hopkins? The hotel heiress? Why was she calling me? Maybe it was a different Alicia Hopkins.

"Yes, hello."

"I was wondering if you would be able to meet with me sometime."

"Regarding what?"

"We have a mutual friend. Jett Draconis."

Of course. Perhaps she was looking for a screenwriter. What had Jett put her up to? *Sure, I'm going to fuck you until you can't see straight, and then to ease my own guilty conscience, I'm going to set you up on a bunch of potential projects.*

"Jett and I aren't exactly friends," I said. "What is it that I can help you with, Ms. Hopkins?"

"Call me Alicia. I just have some information I thought you might be interested in."

"What kind of information?"

"Nothing that I want to discuss over the phone. Are you free for dinner this evening?"

Free? It was Sunday, and I didn't have a shift at the diner. Why not? "Sure. Just tell me where you'll be."

♦ ♦ ♦ ♦

"You seem to have caught Jett's attention." Alicia Hopkins, her frosted tips held perfectly in place with what must have been shellac, smiled and took a sip of what appeared to be a dirty martini with extra olives.

Way to get right to the point. I'd barely sat down. "I'm not sure what you're talking about. But first, why don't you tell me why you asked me here?"

"We'll get to that. First, tell me about your relationship with Jett."

What relationship? We'd had a fuck. It had been amazing. Why would she care anyway? "I don't have a relationship with Jett."

"Sweetheart, I'm not naïve. I know you've been with him."

"Look. I don't mean to be rude, but I fail to see what business any of this is of yours."

"You have a bitchy side." She laughed. "I can see why he has a thing for you."

"I assure you that Jett doesn't have any type of thing for me." No shit. He'd basically kicked me out of his bed this morning. Not that I was going to volunteer that information.

"I've known Jett a long time, Heather," she said, her tone serious. "He has an angle with everything he does."

"I don't doubt that." And I didn't.

"So you do know him, then."

"That's not what I said. But I know how celebrities are. I've been living here for five years."

"I feel there's something I need to tell you, woman to woman," she said.

"What might that be?"

Before she could answer, the waiter appeared at our table. "Would you like something to drink, ma'am?" he asked me, and then nodded to Alicia's nearly empty martini glass. "Can I get you another?"

Alicia drained what was left of her drink. "Yes, please." She popped the remaining two olives into her mouth.

He turned back to me. "And for you?"

"Bring me what she's having." It was definitely going to be a martini kind of evening.

After he left, Alicia said, "Now, where were we?"

"There's something you wanted to tell me. Woman to woman," I couldn't resist adding.

"Yes, of course. I've known Jett a long time. He and I are... How can I put this? More than friends."

So the rock star was sleeping with the heiress. I couldn't say I was surprised. Even though, my heart broke just a little bit. Okay, a lot. I had fallen in love with a womanizer. I strained my face to remain nonchalant, wishing I had my martini in front of me.

"Oh? He didn't mention you." That wasn't even a lie.

I didn't doubt anything she was telling me, but I wanted to smack myself silly for letting on that I had spent more than just a passing moment with him.

"Jett is usually very discreet. And so am I."

"You are? Then why are you telling me about your relationship?"

Her painted cheeks flushed a slightly darker crimson than the blush she'd apparently applied with a palette knife. Other than that giveaway, though, she maintained her composure.

"I can tell, just from the short time we've been talking, that you are also a very discreet person, Heather."

"Really? From spending all of three minutes with me?"

She reached across the table and grabbed my hand. "Come now. Let's just have some girl talk. Get to know each other."

I snatched my hand away. This was getting creepy. "Why? I don't mean to be rude, but what possible interest could you have in me? I'm just a struggling screenwriter."

"You don't have to be struggling."

I saw where this was going. "If you intend to offer to have some big producer read my work in exchange for staying away from Jett, you don't need to bother. Jett and I mean nothing to each other. I won't be seeing him again."

"I can see you have the wrong idea about me. But I would advise you not to burn any bridges. You don't want me as an enemy."

"What bridge could I possibly burn? You don't know anything about me, and there's no need to try to get me to stay away from Jett. I'll do that all on my own. Of course I don't want you as an enemy. I don't want anyone as an enemy. Why would that even be on the table? I'm just saying that..." What was I saying? I had really jumped the gun, and she was right about burning bridges. She knew everyone in LA, and she was probably a good person to have on my side. "I apologize, Alicia. I guess I'm just used to everyone in Hollywood wanting to make a deal, you know?"

She smiled and nodded, taking a sip of the new martini the waiter had placed in front of her. "I accept your apology, of course." She flagged the waiter before he left. "Could you take a photo of us?" She turned back to me. "For my Instagram account. My followers love knowing my every move."

"Uh...sure." Showing up on Alicia Hopkins's Instagram certainly couldn't hurt a struggling screenwriter.

She leaned across the table and put her arm around me as if we were besties. I forced a smile.

The waiter handed Alicia her phone and then strode off.

The whole act felt really strange. Something was definitely up. I just had no idea what it could possibly be.

"So there *is* a reason why I asked you here," she said.

"And that is?" I took a sip of my own drink, wincing at its strength. This was a real martini. Gin, not vodka. It burned my throat, but in a good way.

"Like I said, I've known Jett a long time, and I recognize his MO. What I'm about to tell you won't make the news, but it's the truth. The alleged bomb threat at the Emerald Phoenix concert was a hoax."

"That doesn't surprise me," I said.

"Of course not. But what *may* surprise you is who orchestrated it."

"Oh? Do you know who did?"

"Yes. Jett did." She fiddled with her phone.

I arched my eyebrows and my heart quickened. "Why would he stage a fake bomb threat at his own concert? That doesn't make sense."

"Oh, it does, and it's not the first time he's done something like this. He did it because he wanted to fuck you, Heather."

CHAPTER NINETEEN

JETT

After rehearsal, I joined the guys and others close to the band for an early dinner at Zane's place. Of course he'd also invited several groupies to join us. I cornered our agent, Miranda Carson, to find out news.

"Anything on the bomb threat?"

She shook her head. "The bomb squad swept the place and didn't uncover anything. It was obviously a hoax, but we don't have any idea who perpetrated it."

My heart thumped. This wasn't the first bomb hoax we'd dealt with, but this time had affected me differently.

Heather had been there.

I wanted to know who had done this, who had made me think Heather was in danger. I wanted to know so I could make him pay and pay dearly. I'd start by kicking the shit out of him.

Janet must have been busy because Lindy was getting busy with a redhead on Zane's leather couch.

Redhead.

This woman's hair was clearly out of a bottle, and her tits looked like two cereal bowls sticking straight out. Yup, fake.

The only redhead I wanted was Heather's natural auburn.

Her tits sure weren't fake. They were fucking perfect.

I looked over at Zane. Man, the dude was never going to grow up. Hard to believe that this was actually Zeb Frankfurter, classical pianist and notorious nerdy introvert who five years ago had been afraid of women. Alicia had remade him. Turned out that with a gym regimen, Lasik surgery, and a blond dye job, Z was a pretty boy chick magnet. He no longer had to fear women. Hell, they flocked to him in gaggles.

All she'd done for me was add some hair extensions. They'd grown out long ago. I'd always had a muscular physique, and now, with three workouts a week and the physical activity of rehearsal and performing, I maintained it easily. There was a lot more of Jeremy in me than Zeb in Zane. Whether that was good or bad? I didn't know.

But Alicia had done a lot more than change our appearances. She'd initiated our spiral to the top.

It had come at a cost.

Much more for me than for Zane.

My phone vibrated against my hip. I grabbed it and looked at the screen.

Speak of the devil. A text from Alicia, accompanied by a photo.

Look who came to dinner.

Alicia...with Heather. And I recognized the restaurant.

Damn her!

If she'd told Heather...

I stood and walked out of Zane's rec room. No one noticed me leave. They were too busy watching Lindy's show with the redhead.

Then another phone buzz.

I want you in my bed tonight.

Damn her to hell!

I looked around Zane's mansion, which was even bigger and more ridiculous than my own. Z would never go back to being a classical pianist. He was all in and too far gone. This was his life now.

But me?

During the last year, I'd begun to wonder if it had all been worth it. I'd sold my soul for fame and fortune. And now?

I was stuck between a rock and a hard place. I'd fallen in love with a woman I could never have. She could never know I loved her, and my chance at true happiness would fade away like the sunset at dusk. All because I'd signed a deal with the devil.

I didn't want to go to Alicia's, but I knew what would happen if I didn't.

One thing was for sure. She was going to tell me exactly what she'd been doing with Heather Myles at that restaurant. In fact, I'd go to that restaurant and see for myself. And that would also be the last time she'd ever see Heather.

Unfortunately, it was probably the last time I'd see Heather as well.

CHAPTER TWENTY

HEATHER

"Excuse me?"

"I'm sure there's nothing wrong with your ears, Heather. Jett orchestrated that fake bomb threat so he could rush off the stage, sweep you off your feet, and"—she made air quote marks—"*save* you."

I stared at Alicia, my mouth agape.

"This isn't the first time he's pulled a stunt like this. He's never resorted to a bomb threat in the past, but he'll go to any length to get a woman he wants into his bed. Usually all it takes is a couple of fucks in one night to get it out of his system."

I forced my lips together. As much as I didn't want to admit it to myself, Alicia's words were ringing true. He'd pursued me. I rebuffed him. Then he faked the bomb threat to gain my trust. He fucked me. Then he kicked me out of his bed.

I'd fallen right into it.

"I'm sorry, honey. Have I upset you?" She smiled, and saccharine oozed from her pores.

I cleared my throat and took another sip of my strong drink. "Why would any of that upset me?" I said, hoping I sounded a lot more indifferent than I felt.

"Jett is an attractive and successful man. Every woman wants to be his one and only."

"I'm not every woman."

"No, you're not. I can tell you're a lot smarter than the trash he usually lures into his bed." She smiled again, her teeth so white I nearly had to shield my eyes.

"I'd like to think so," I said. "But truly, there's nothing going on between Jett and me."

"It's good that you have that attitude," Alicia said. "I'd hate to see him hurt you. A few women have fallen in love with him along the way. He's broken some hearts. I'd hate to see him break yours."

"I assure you that won't happen." No, it wouldn't happen, because it already had. I pushed my drink across the table. "I'm really not hungry, and I'm on deadline. I think it's best if I leave."

"You can't leave!" she said adamantly, reaching across the table and grasping my hand again.

Her touch burned, and not in a good way.

"Let go of me," I said, my nerves jumping.

"I'm sorry." She let go of my hand. "But please, stay. I invited you for a meal, and I always keep my word."

I sighed. A girl had to eat. She didn't seem to have an ulterior motive other than keeping Jett to herself. I wasn't the least bit hungry—not after the news she'd given me—but I didn't want to be rude. Alicia Hopkins was not a bridge I wanted to burn. She knew all the top producers in Hollywood.

I forced a smile. "Of course. Thank you for the invitation. I'm happy to stay and eat." I picked up my menu. "What's good here?"

"The filet mignon is to die for. And the chef's special of the day is always something unique and delicious."

The filet mignon was the most expensive thing on the menu. No way was I ordering it, even though Alicia Hopkins could easily afford it. I looked for something innocuous, something that said I have taste, but I'm also frugal. Also, something that would not stain my shirt when I undoubtedly dropped a bite due to nervousness. "I think I'll have the penne carbonara, unless the chef's special is something I can't live without."

"You don't want to try the filet?"

"I don't eat a lot of red meat." What a big lie. I was a carnivore of the highest order.

"That's too bad. It truly is amazing." Alicia didn't pick up her menu but took the last sip of her second martini. Then her smile widened. "Oh my, look who it is!" She stood. "Over here, Jett, darling."

Nausea threatened in my throat, and I knew. Alicia had planned all of this. It was all too...convenient.

Warmth crept up my cheeks, and I knew they were turning pink. I was no actress, but I was determined to play the part of the woman who didn't give a damn. The woman who was *not* in love with Jett Draconis.

It didn't help that he looked absolutely magnificent. His long hair was up in a messy man bun, and he had a day's worth of stubble on his cheeks and chin. I had seen the beginning of that stubble this morning...

No. I was not going there. Time to turn on the charm. I

forced another smile.

Alicia stood and wrapped her arms around Jett's neck. "What are you doing here?" She turned to look at me. "I guess I don't need to introduce you to my dinner companion. You obviously know Heather, since you carried her out of the concert hall last night during the bomb threat."

Without meaning to, I let my gaze meet Jett's. His hazel eyes were sharp, and they glittered with something I hadn't seen in them before. Was it anger? Was he angry with me?

That couldn't be. I hadn't done anything to invoke his anger. He was the one who had kicked *me* out of his bed.

I waited for him to say hello. To say *something*.

Alicia pulled him to our table. "You must join us for dinner. We haven't even ordered yet. Here, you can sit by me."

The way she was gushing over him made my guts boil. A spear of jealousy shot into my body. Alicia Hopkins had slept with Jett. No surprise there, but it was written all over her face.

I couldn't figure out exactly what was written on Jett's face. His eyes still glittered with what I thought was anger, but also a bit of... Was it sorrow?

Before he sat down, he looked at Alicia. "Can I talk to you in private please?"

"Later. I've asked Heather to dinner, and you wouldn't want me to be rude, would you?"

I opened my mouth, hoping my words wouldn't come out in a stammer. "If you'll excuse me, I'll just go to the ladies room for a few minutes. Then you can talk to each other."

"I wouldn't dream of having you leave on our account," Alicia said.

"It's okay, really. I do need to use the ladies room." God, did I ever. I wasn't the least bit sure I could keep my martini from coming back out the way it had gone in. I left the table in a hurry.

When I got to the ladies room, I walked down to the last stall, entered, locked it, and then leaned against the wall, breathing hard. *Calm down, Heather. This is nothing. You can deal with it.* When my breathing didn't slow down, I grabbed a paper bag from the dispenser for disposing sanitary supplies and breathed into it. In about a minute, I had reversed the hyperventilation.

I had to go back out there. I had no choice. Like an idiot, I'd left my purse at the table, so I couldn't sneak out of the restaurant. Not that I would have anyway. I'd hate myself if I did. Plus, what better way to show Jett Draconis I was fine with his treatment of me than to go back out with a smile on my face and chat animatedly about...well, anything.

Never mind that I wasn't sure I'd ever chatted animatedly in my life. Time to learn.

When I felt I had a grip on myself, I left the stall, washed my hands, and assessed my appearance in the mirror. My lipstick was still okay, since all I'd had so far was a drink. I would do. Of course, I couldn't help wishing that I looked like... well, like a rock star, and that Jett would be sorry he ever let me go.

When I reentered the dining room, I looked over to our table. Jett still hadn't sat down. He was conversing with Alicia from a standing position.

I inhaled and let out my breath slowly. Then I walked

toward the table.

And stopped abruptly when—

"You fucking bitch!" Jett shouted to Alicia.

CHAPTER TWENTY-ONE

JETT

"What the fuck are you doing?" I said in an urgent whisper.

"Taking a promising young screenwriter to dinner. What are you doing here?"

"You knew I'd come when I got your photo. Stop the games, Alicia. What are you after?"

"Just a little reminder. Remember who made you, who you belong to, and what can happen if you betray me."

"Don't you pull that shit with me. We had a deal. I could sleep with whoever I wanted."

"Yes, we do have that deal. But you are also mine, and I don't want you to forget that."

"What makes you think I forgot that?" God knew I hadn't. And God knew I wished I could, now that I had actually fallen in love.

"Your little redheaded slut."

"She means nothing to me." The lie tasted terrible, like stomach acid and bad wine. I felt like I needed to wash my mouth out with soap like my mother had when I was a kid.

"You really think I'm stupid, don't you? You risked your

life last night. You jumped off the stage when I know damned well you were told to leave the back way."

"I don't know what you're talking about."

"Don't you? You jumped off the stage to rescue the little redhead."

"I was acting on instinct." That wasn't even a lie. My instinct was to get Heather out of there safely.

"I don't buy it. But don't worry. I took care of it."

"What did you do?" I said through clenched teeth.

"Oh, nothing much. I simply told her that *you* orchestrated the bomb threat so you could save her and get her into your bed. It worked, didn't it?"

"You fucking bitch!"

"Lower your voice," Alicia scolded. "Heather is coming back."

I looked toward the restrooms. Heather stood, her mouth dropped open. I didn't know how much she had heard, but she had at least heard me call Alicia a bitch. I didn't want to upset Heather, but I couldn't bring myself to be sorry the words had left my mouth.

Alicia smiled and looked at Heather. She motioned for her to come forward.

Heather walked slowly, biting her lower lip. God, she was so beautiful. She didn't deserve any of this. She didn't deserve to be a part of my fucked-up world.

She sat down as if nothing were amiss and then took a drink of the martini in front of her. Her cheeks were pink, her lips were red, her long auburn hair was in a bit of disarray around her shoulders. She was wearing a peach-colored camisole, and her nipples protruded through, as if asking me to bite them through the silk.

I was still so fucking angry, yet my groin tightened.

I took a seat next to Heather, and Alicia looked at me with poison in her gaze.

The waiter came to take our order. Heather robotically ordered some sort of pasta, and I ordered the filet mignon and a bottle of their best Bordeaux. Alicia might never pay for what she was putting Heather through, but she would at least pay for a rock star dinner.

"So..." Alicia began. "Any news on the bomb threat?"

Heather arched her eyebrows at Alicia. I opened my mouth to tell Heather that Alicia had fed her a pack of lies, but then Alicia arched her eyebrows at me.

Somehow, I had to figure out how to let Heather know that Alicia had lied to her. But how could I? The bomb squad and the cops hadn't uncovered anything about the bomb, so there was nothing I could say.

"Not yet," I said. "The bomb squad thinks it was a hoax, same as the one in Philadelphia." There, that should help. I hadn't rushed off the stage to rescue anyone in Philadelphia. Plus, I was telling the damned truth.

Heather took another drink of her martini. If only I could get her alone. Make her understand what kind of person Alicia was. Tell her I'd had nothing to do with the phony bomb threat.

And then it hit me. Alicia herself had orchestrated the threat. Who else? Somehow, she had figured out I was interested in Heather.

If only I could turn the tables on Alicia and prove that

she had been behind the bomb threat. If I were the only one at risk, I wouldn't hesitate. But I *wasn't* the only one at risk. Two people I loved dearly would go down if I did.

Alicia Hopkins was the worst kind of evil. She had grown up with a platinum spoon in her mouth and was used to buying everything she wanted as an adult.

Like an idiot, I had let her buy me.

Heather was moving in a stiff way, as if a cape of frost blanketed her. I could easily sense her discomfort because I shared it. I remained stiff as a board when all I wanted to do was turn, grab Heather, and kiss her.

I didn't usually mind silence, but this silence was icy and awkward. Alicia chatted on and on about some charity benefit or another. The words sounded like a garbled radio signal. I was thankful when we had all finished and the waiter brought the check.

Out of habit, I reached for it, forgetting for a minute that I wanted Alicia to pay.

"It's my treat." Alicia swept the check to her side of the table. "I'm the one who invited Heather here, after all."

"Yes, and I can't thank you enough." She rose. "But if you'll excuse me, I do need to be going."

I stood. "I'll walk you out."

But Alicia had other plans for me. "No, Jett. Please stay. I have something I really need to discuss with you. I was going to call you later, but since you're here..."

She had told me she wanted me in her bed. Alicia was not one to back down. So I would fuck her tonight—not that I had a choice—and figure out what to do about Heather tomorrow.

An odd emotion enveloped me as I watched Heather walk away from our table for the exit.

She didn't look back at me. Not once. Not that I expected her to. She certainly didn't owe me anything. And then it hit me like an asteroid hitting the earth. That emotion I was feeling. It was loss. Profound loss.

Out of the restaurant marched my one shot at happiness in this life.

When I was twenty-five years old, I hadn't given a thought to tomorrow. Zane and I were a package deal with Alicia. She would take us both to the top in exchange for...basically indentured servitude. We could fuck whomever we liked as long as we made ourselves available to her as an escort—or more often a fuck—whenever she demanded it. Not falling in love wasn't an actual part of the deal with Alicia, but what woman would agree to let us fuck another woman whenever she called? Falling in love was off the table.

Zane's situation and mine were not identical, however. He could walk away whenever he felt like it. She didn't have anything on him to control him besides her promise to keep him at the top, which was enough for him. I required a little more. So Alicia had dived into my past and found a secret my family and I had hoped to keep buried forever.

Alicia scribbled her name on the credit card receipt and then turned to me. "Shall we go?"

I stood. "Yeah."

Might as well get it over with.

♦ ♦ ♦ ♦

She wanted to be tied up tonight. Tied up and whipped hard across her ass and thighs. She particularly liked it when I left marks. Once she was good and bruised, she liked to be fucked hard, first in the pussy and then the ass.

As much as I had grown to hate Alicia, I didn't like leaving marks on her body. Though I loved playing the dominant role in the bedroom, hurting someone to the point of marring her body felt abusive to me. But she demanded it, so I complied.

She had a dungeon in her mansion that made mine look like a child's play area.

I knew what she required, so I sucked in a breath and began.

"Undress, bitch."

"Yes, Sir." She smiled and slowly stripped for me.

Although she was well into her fifties, Alicia was a great-looking woman with a smoking-hot body—lots of liposuction and Botox. I had stopped finding her attractive about a year ago, though, when I had begun to regret the deal I had made with her. Still, fucking her had been no hardship, and I had never imagined I would fall in love, so I continued.

Right now, though? I wasn't sure I could get an erection.

Alicia's pussy was freshly waxed, her clit ring dangling.

"Go to the wall," I commanded. "Get me the black snake whip."

Her body flushed pink. "Yes, Sir." She turned and walked slowly to the wall.

"Faster, bitch. Bring it to me and then get on your knees."

She obeyed, handing me the leather whip and then kneeling before me.

"Would you like me to suck your cock, Sir?"

That was the last thing I wanted. My poor dick felt like it was going to shrivel up and die. "No. You said you wanted to be whipped. I intend to whip you."

"Oh, yes, Sir. Please whip me hard."

"Don't talk again unless I instruct you to." That was one way to keep her quiet.

She nodded.

"Go to the table and lie facedown."

She complied, and I bound her wrists and ankles to the poles at each corner of the leather-covered table. The hard cowhide of the snake whip was warm in my palm.

Alicia squirmed on the table. "Please, Sir. Spank my ass. I can't wait any longer."

"I told you not to talk. For that, you will wait ten minutes until I touch your body with this whip."

She let out a gasp but did not say another word.

And I got a ten-minute reprieve.

CHAPTER TWENTY-TWO

HEATHER

Exhaustion weighed on my shoulders as I unlocked the door to my apartment. That dinner date had taken more out of me than a ten-mile run. But why should I be surprised? Everything Alicia had told me had made a twisted kind of sense.

I sighed and opened the door, planning to grab a glass of water and head straight to my bedroom.

Those plans went by the wayside when I walked into my apartment and saw Susie on the couch with Janet, the woman I'd found in Jett's bed.

"Oh, good, Heather. You're home," Susie said. "You know Janet, right?"

Janet smiled. "We've met. Great to see you again, Heather."

"Janet actually came over here to talk to you," Susie said.

"Yeah?" I said rather shortly. I didn't mean to be rude, but this woman had been in the bed of the man I had fallen in love with. God only knew how many times they'd fucked.

"Susie and I have known each other for ages," Janet said. "She speaks very highly of you."

"That's nice." *So what?*

"Jett has obviously taken a liking to you," Janet continued. "Susie and I were just talking, and we thought it might be fun if you and I got together to do a show for him."

I raised my brow and then picked up my jaw from the floor.

Janet kept talking. "He loves seeing a black girl and white girl together. It's kind of a fetish of his. And babe, you're hot. I could totally do you."

Speechless. I said nothing.

"Susie said you might be a little resistant. Would it help if I told you that Susie and I have been together?"

"What? No. Christ. I'm not into girls."

Janet and Susie giggled. "That's not what Susie says."

I shot daggers at Susie with my glare. A couple of months ago, after we'd had way too many margaritas, I had confessed to Susie that I had a girl crush on the actress Lupita Nyong'o. She had such exotic beauty, and I loved her dark, flawless skin.

And truthfully, Janet made Lupita look average.

I loved Susie like a sister, but I could already tell the way her mind was working. If I thought Lupita Nyong'o was attractive, surely I would jump at the chance to hop in bed with a woman as gorgeous as Janet.

That was the groupie mentality—fuck whomever you had to in order to get your prey's attention. Never mind that I had no desire to sleep with Lupita Nyong'o. I just thought she was amazing-looking. And I had even less desire to sleep with Janet or Susie or any other woman.

"What I was thinking," Janet went on, "was that the two of us could sneak into his bedroom and surprise him tonight."

"Breaking and entering?" I shook my head. "I don't think I want to get arrested, but thanks."

Janet laughed. "We wouldn't break in, silly."

"Then how would we get into his house?" And why had I just asked that question? It wasn't like I was actually considering this.

"Lindy and I are good friends with his maid. She lets us in whenever we want."

"And Jett's okay with that?"

"Are you kidding? She wouldn't do it if he weren't. She's not going to do anything to jeopardize that cushy job."

"So let me get this straight. You're suggesting that you and I sneak into Jett's bed, and when he gets home we put on a little show for him?" The whole thing sounded absurd to me, but heck, we were in Hollywood. Anything went here.

"That's exactly what I'm suggesting, babe." She winked at me. "Though we can start before he gets there if you'd like. You're fucking hot."

I looked around my living room. No hidden cameras that I could see, though I could've sworn I was on some kind of reality TV show.

"I told Jan that you probably wouldn't want to do this," Susie said. "After all, you wouldn't make out with me after the concert the other night to get his attention."

"I told you. I'm not into girls."

Janet smiled. "Baby, all women are into women. They just don't know it. And honey, I haven't met a man yet who's as good at licking pussy as another woman is. But hey, I get what you're saying. I love a good hard dick as much as the next woman. Right, Suze?"

Susie laughed. "Jan's had more dick than Jenna Jameson."

"Think of our little show as foreplay," Janet said. "That's actually exactly what it is. Then the main attraction is Jett's big cock."

"I'm pretty sure he only has one."

"So what are *you* going to do while he's fucking me? Is that what you're asking?" Janet let out a raucous laugh. "Baby, while he's pounding me, I'm going to have my long tongue so far up your cunt that you're going to cream all over my face." She slid what indeed appeared to be an oddly long tongue over her full, dusky lips.

My clit started to throb. I couldn't deny being intrigued. Was I actually considering this? I already knew Jett Draconis was a douche. At least my head did. My heart had fallen hopelessly in love with the jerk.

But oh my God... To be able to relive at least part of being with Jett. How in sync we had been, how his skin had felt against mine, how his hard cock had felt plunging inside me...

If fooling around with Janet in Jett's bed could get me just a few more minutes in his presence...

This was so fucked up. Janet was attractive, and I was intrigued—especially after seeing her tongue. But to do this *just* to have more time with Jett? I couldn't. Just couldn't.

So I wasn't sure why the next words out of my mouth were, "Sounds like fun. Let's do it."

CHAPTER TWENTY-THREE

JETT

Normally, ten minutes goes by very slowly when you're just watching the second hand. However, when you're in a situation that you want to put off as long as possible, ten minutes goes by in a flash.

I raised the whip and brought it down hard on the back of Alicia's thighs. She squealed. This was normal for her, but because I didn't want to hear any part of her, I said, "Be quiet. One more sound out of you, and I'll wait another ten minutes."

I brought the whip down upon her thighs again. No noise out of her this time, though she did wince.

Whip! Whip! Whip!

Three more times upon her thighs. They were reddening, so I moved to the cheeks of her ass.

Whip! Whip! Whip!

Her ass reddened as well. Much more, and I'd leave marks. I brought it down on her ass once more.

She wanted to be fucked now. I could tell. The smell of her arousal wafted thickly in the air. Doughy bread and earth, nothing like the sweet fresh apples and musk of Heather's scent.

I wasn't even slightly hard.

I gave her a few lashes on her back to hold her over, and then I picked up a blindfold from a nearby table. I secured it over her eyes so she couldn't watch what I was doing next.

"Stay quiet," I commanded. "Not a peep out of you. I will come to you when I'm ready."

I quietly riffled through a box of dildos until I found one that was about the size of my own cock. I couldn't help smiling. It was one of the biggest in the box. Then I undressed. My dick was still limp. I hastily put a condom over the dildo to make it feel more realistic to her.

"Get ready. I'm going to shove my hard cock in your tight little cunt, Alicia."

She didn't speak, only bit her lip and sighed.

She was wet so it was easy to plunge the dildo into her pussy.

She let out a low moan.

I fucked her hard with the dildo, grazing my free hand and forearm against her thighs to make it seem more real, creating guttural moans in my throat.

"You can talk now," I said. "Tell me how my big dick feels inside you."

"Baby, no one feels like you do inside me. You have the biggest cock in the universe."

Nothing I hadn't heard from Alicia before. A time had existed when her words had made me feel like some kind of god. Now? I just wanted this to be over with so I could figure out how I could fix my stupid life.

"God, baby, so good. You fuck me so good."

I rolled my eyes. "I'm going to come. I'm going to unload inside you."

"But my ass..."

"Not today. I want to come in that hot pussy of yours."

She let out a low moan. "Yes, please come, baby. Come all over me."

"Yeah, yeah," I said, grunting. "Here I come." I thrust the dildo hard into her while I faked the orgasm. Damn, should have been an actor.

"Keep that blindfold on," I commanded as I pulled the dildo out of her and disposed of the wet condom.

None of that had turned me on at all. My cock still hung flaccid between my legs. I quietly placed the dildo back in the box.

The black snake whip sat on the table where I'd left it. I hung it back up on the wall.

Still naked, I took the blindfold off of her.

She smiled as she gazed at me. "I'll never get tired of looking at you naked, baby. You are one fine man."

I forced a smile.

"I hope you left some good marks on me."

I hadn't, but I said, "Of course."

"No one whips me like you do. You have a strong and forceful hand. And then that big cock of yours..." She stared at the limp member between my legs. "Wow. I really took it out of you this time."

Another forced smile. "You always do."

She was relaxed and sated. Time for me to move in for the kill.

"Hey, sweetheart," I said. "Could you do me a favor?"

"Anything, doll."

"Leave Heather Myles alone. She's a nice kid, just a struggling screenwriter trying to make it."

She smiled. "I'll leave her alone if you will, darling."

It took every ounce of strength I had to nod. "Of course. I have no interest in her."

♦ ♦ ♦ ♦

Driving home from Alicia's place hadn't given me any epiphanies about how to get out of my deal with the LA devil.

That was Jeremy's problem. I was Jett now. Jett was a superstar. He could get out of anything. So I had to think like Jett.

Problem was, Jett would do what was best for Jett, and fuck the fallout.

Jett didn't fall in love, so Jett never had to worry about fallout.

Jett was also an illusion.

Jeremy had fallen in love with Heather Myles, and Jeremy was the one who had to protect his loved ones from Alicia.

Man, I needed a drink. Neither alcohol nor drugs had ever been huge habits of mine, but right now a stiff bourbon sounded good. Anything to take the edge off.

Fucking Heather would take the edge off, but that wouldn't—*couldn't*—happen again. Not until I'd figured out how to get out of the bear trap holding me down.

The only way was to chew my own leg off.

Chew my own leg off...

I walked up the stairs to my bedroom, my mind churning. There had to be a way to get my leg out of the trap, to chew it off without taking others down. I'd happily live without a metaphorical leg to be free from Alicia and her manipulation.

I opened the door, walked in to the sitting area, pulled the band out of my hair, and then—

I jerked my head toward my bed.

It hadn't been my imagination.

Auburn tresses were splayed out on my sheets.

Auburn tresses I'd last seen a few hours earlier in the restaurant with Alicia. They'd been in a ponytail then.

Auburn tresses I'd recognize anywhere.

I ran toward the bed. "Heath—"

A head of ebony hair poked upward.

Janet.

In my bed.

Not so surprising. I'd found her there countless times before.

But not with Heather.

Heather wasn't a groupie. Heather was better than this.

What the fuck?

"Hey, babe," Janet said, her voice low and husky. "We thought you'd *never* get here."

CHAPTER TWENTY-FOUR

HEATHER

I jerked my head over my shoulder.

Jett. His hair was wild in disarray, and his hazel eyes burned.

The core of my body warmed and shot tingles through the rest of me. Yes, the man was a supreme douchebag, but somehow, even though I knew this, I still wanted him.

God help me, I still loved him.

I was an intelligent person, an educated person, a person who believed in being the best I could be. Why the hell couldn't I see past Jett's charisma?

I'd fallen in love with a fantasy. After he'd told me about his music education and his love of opera, I'd created the Jett I wanted him to be in my mind. I'd fallen in love with that creation.

Simple enough. What I loved didn't exist.

But I could still have one more time with his miraculous body, even if I had to screw a girl to get it.

It had been several seconds since Janet had spoken, yet Jett said nothing. He just stared at me, looking like a black wolf in the wild.

"Looks like he needs a little incentive," Janet said flirtatiously. "Spread those long legs, babe. I can't wait to taste the treats between them."

This was really happening. A girl was going to go down on me. Not just any girl, but a gorgeous one with a foot-long tongue.

Janet had wanted to get busy before Jett got there, but I'd begged off. "It'll be better if we save it." Yeah, right. I was just too afraid to get started. Truly, this wasn't my thing, and now I had a woman between my legs, her tongue slithering up the slit of my pussy.

And God, it felt fucking good.

She licked my clit, flicking the point of her tongue over it, and my nipples hardened. Then she swirled down through my folds and shoved that long tongue into my wet heat.

Fuck! I grasped at the bed linens, wanting to grind into her face but stopping myself. I still wasn't sure I should be doing this. I was holding back.

But why?

It felt good, so why not go with it?

So I let my fingers wander over my breasts to my turgid nipples, and I squeezed.

God!

Jett's gaze intensified.

Had I said that out loud?

Yes, I must have.

Janet was right about being able to suck my pussy like a champ, but still...

She wasn't as good as Jett had been.

I forced that thought from my mind and concentrated on pleasuring my aching nipples.

"You like it, babe?" Janet said between my thighs, her full lips glistening. "I suck your pussy nice, right? Didn't I tell you?"

All I could do was moan and twist my nipples harder.

She had me on the edge of an orgasm, but I didn't feel right about it. So I held back and just enjoyed the sensation of her sucking between my legs, my own fingers pleasuring my hard nubs.

Until Jett finally reanimated.

He moved quickly to where Janet was lying and rolled her over.

"Sorry, Jan. That pussy's mine."

And then...heaven. His tongue wasn't as long as Janet's, but it was rougher and wider. And as soon as it touched my clit, I burst into orgasm.

"Yeah, baby. You come for me." He forced two fingers into my channel. "You come for me. Only me."

Janet slid up the bed and took over pleasuring one of my nipples. She clamped her full, dark lips around one and sucked hard.

Damn, that felt good.

But all I could do was watch Jett's wild mane as he worked my pussy.

"You're not done coming," he said. "I want another orgasm, Heather. And then I want another. I want you to come so fast and hard that you can't take any more. And when you finally get to that point, I'm going to make you come once more."

Warmth spread through me as fire ignited in my veins.

Janet let my nipple drop. "You like how he eats your pussy, babe?"

"God, yes," I moaned.

"You're pink all over, babe," she said. "You're so hot. And you have great breasts. Mmm." She took my other nipple between her lips.

Jett continued to work my flesh, and then he lifted my hips and slid his tongue over my asshole.

So forbidden, yet so perfect.

He continued to move two fingers in and out of my pussy, and then—

"Ah!"

He breached my tight rim.

"Easy, baby. I told you, you're not done coming." And his lips clamped back down on my clit.

"Feels good in the ass, doesn't it?" Janet said.

Then her mouth came down on mine.

Her lips were soft, softer than any man's, and her long tongue swept into my mouth, velvety and smooth.

Again, it was nothing like kissing Jett, but while he had his mouth and hands tied up with my pussy, being able to enjoy a kiss was a sweet extra I found myself liking.

I loved kissing. I loved the feeling of tongues and lips sliding together. I loved tasting the mouth of another person. Janet tasted sweet, like a fruity mint. My tongue met hers, and the kiss went deeper.

I groaned into her mouth as Jett pulled another orgasm out of me, and then another.

I was so sated, so purely in the moment. Getting to kiss while a tongue and two hands pleasured my pussy.

Heaven. Pure bliss.

Until Janet broke our kiss.

"Mmm, I'm so horny, babe. So wet. I'm going to sit on your face."

I opened my mouth to say no, but Jett forced another climax from my weary body. I cried out, and before I knew it, I had a face full of Janet's pussy.

She didn't set her weight onto me, just squatted over my mouth.

She was letting me go at my pace. It was up to me to begin.

Again, I thought of refusing, but Jett pulled one last explosive climax from me, and my tongue, as if of its own volition, shot out and touched Janet's dark pussy lips.

It was soft beneath my tongue, with a tang of citrus and sex.

"Don't be afraid, babe. Just do what feels nice." Janet said above me.

Nerves jittered through me. I tried tonguing her again, but this time fear got to me. I wasn't ready for this. Didn't want to do this.

Whether he sensed it, I didn't know, but Jett came to my rescue.

"I want to kiss her sweet mouth, Jan." He lifted Janet off my face and replaced her with his firm full lips laced with my own flavor.

And in that moment, I knew I had made the right decision to come back to Jett's bed. I had needed to experience his kiss one more time, feel his lips sliding against my own, his tongue swirling inside my mouth. I had enjoyed kissing Janet. I had enjoyed kissing many other men in the past. But Jett...

No kisses compared to his.

If he'd truly rigged a bomb threat just to have me, well, then, I'd let him have me. And I'd get to have him at the same time. Win-win situation.

I wasn't sure what Janet was doing. Jett was on top of me and still fully clothed. She couldn't get to his cock. She couldn't get anywhere on me either, because Jett was covering me. I closed my eyes and lost myself in the moment. I didn't care where Janet was. All thoughts flew from my head and only pure emotion remained. I was kissing the man I loved. No, he didn't love me, but that was okay.

Right now, everything was perfect.

Fragmented images flooded my mind, releasing me from all cognitive thought. Abstract red, pink—the colors of love— swirling in images of hearts and clouds. My nipples were hard, poking into Jett's still-clothed chest.

Yet still we kissed, and though my nipples and my pussy craved his touch, I didn't want to stop the embrace. If it was to be the last time I kissed him, I wanted to draw it out as long as I could.

But too soon, he broke the kiss. I whimpered with loss when he pulled his mouth from mine. He gazed at me for a moment, his brown-green eyes dark with smoke and fire. Time seemed to stop as we looked at each other, making love to each other through our vision.

But then he turned his head.

"Jan, sweetheart, why don't you have Lars drive you home? I want to be alone with my girl."

My girl. The words flowed over me like warm chocolate syrup. *My girl.*

Of course it meant nothing, but while I was here—in his bed, in his arms—I could pretend it meant something not just to me, but to him. As if he really meant those words that broke forth from his throat in his deep husky voice.

My girl.

My pussy gushed fresh juice, aching for his hard cock.

Had Janet answered him? I didn't know. I lost all sense of time in the present when he uttered those words. *My girl.*

If only this could last forever. If only...

Jett turned back toward me, gazing down at me again, intensity in his eyes. He opened his mouth but didn't say anything. Only his tongue emerged, and I let my own out to meet his. They touched softly—only our tongues, no lips—tasting each other. Feeling our tongues swirl together tightened my nipples even more. It was beautiful. Hot and beautiful.

Then I closed my eyes and surrendered to the moment.

Our tongues tangled together for a few minutes more, and then Jett closed the gap and our lips touched for a deep, long kiss. It was a frantic kiss, the kiss of two souls who had longed for each other.

At least that's how it felt to me.

I would go with my fantasy for now. I would enjoy the hell out of this last encounter with Jett. I would make it count. If I never had another encounter that equaled it, that would be okay, because I'd had this one.

His hard cock pressed against my belly and pubic bone. It was still encased in his jeans, and I longed for it to be set free. He was still clothed on top of me, and I was naked. Being naked with him didn't bother me, but I desperately wanted him naked too, to feel his skin against mine, let our warmth mingle together.

He groaned, vibrating into my mouth and throat. I answered with a soft moan of my own, our lips still sliding against each other's, our tongues still dueling.

God, this kiss. This unending kiss...

But then...it ended.

His blazing eyes gazed into mine. "Turn over, baby. Get on your hands and knees."

Disobeying him never occurred to me. I turned quickly, even though I longed not to lose the eye contact. My nipples were aching for his touch, but obviously he had other plans.

I closed my eyes, breathing in and then exhaling. What did he have in store for me?

He slid his wet tongue over my asshole. "Have you ever been fucked in the ass, Heather?"

I whimpered but said nothing.

"Have you ever had anal sex, baby? Your ass is so beautiful. I want to shove my cock deep inside you. Show you something new."

At that moment, I would've given Jett anything. So I did.

"No, I haven't. But I want you to be my first."

CHAPTER TWENTY-FIVE

JETT

Thank God. If she had turned me down, I'd have still fucked her into oblivion. Fucked her until she couldn't walk. But I *wanted* that asshole, and now that I knew it was a virgin, my cock was harder than it had ever been.

I took a few seconds to hastily shed my clothing and throw it on a nearby chair. Then I went back and stuck my face between Heather's gorgeous legs. I took a moment to inhale, to smell the fragrance she had created for me. I'd already had quite a fill of her pussy, but I couldn't help shoving my tongue into her wetness once more. She was sweet—sweetest pussy I'd ever tasted. If this was the last chance I got to savor every bit of her, I wasn't going to waste the moment.

She moaned softly into the pillow, and her sounds only fueled my desire. I sucked and bit at her pussy lips, sucked and bit at her hard little clit. She was everything I had ever wanted, ever dreamed of—this intelligent, beautiful woman with more integrity than anyone in LA should be allowed to have.

More integrity than *I* had.

The truth was...I wasn't nearly good enough for Heather Myles.

She deserved someone who could give her what she was worthy of—marriage, children...a lifetime.

How I wanted to give all of those to her—things I never dreamed I would want. Now that I'd met Heather, the desire for those basics ached within me.

Just thinking of a life with her, of making children with her, made my dick throb harder.

But I had to get her ready first.

"You're so sweet, baby," I said against her wet folds. "You respond to me so beautifully. You get so wet for me."

"Please," she said into the pillow. "Please."

I wasn't sure what she was asking for, but I would give her an orgasm. I nipped at her clit and shoved two of my fingers into her pussy. She erupted around me, convulsing against my fingers in a beautiful rhythm.

"That's it, baby. Come for me. Come all over my hand."

She undulated her hips, pushing backward onto my fingers, juicing all over me.

Fuck, I wanted her. I couldn't have her ass just yet. Had to have that sweet little pussy around my cock. I pushed into her balls deep.

"Ah!" she cried out, her voice muffled in the pillow.

I let out a long, slow groan. Such sweet suction. I damn near exploded right there. But I held myself. I was going to come in that sweet tight ass of hers. She was already well-lubed from the pussy and ass licking I'd given her. I swirled the juices around her asshole before probing with my index finger.

She gasped.

"Easy, baby. Just a finger. I'll get you ready first."

Her hole was tight and warm around the tip of my finger. Maybe I'd just finger her tonight. Her pussy felt so good around me, and I wanted to come so badly.

But I had to hold back. Had to. This might be the last time I ever had her naked under me, and I needed every moment to count.

I stuck my finger all the way into her tight hole. "Feel good, baby?"

"God, yes," she whimpered into the pillow.

"Easy. Yeah, take my whole finger, baby. You're so wet."

I worked a second finger into her. She fisted the covers, but didn't gasp this time.

"That's it. Easy. That's two fingers, baby. You're almost ready for my hard cock. God, I want you so much. I want to shove my cock so far into your ass that we both see stars. Damn, baby."

She was a trouper, taking my fingers like a champ. I could hardly believe she had never had anal sex before. But she hadn't. Heather would never lie to me.

"You ready for my cock, baby?"

She nodded.

"You sure?"

"Yes, Jett. I'm so very sure."

Damn, my balls were already scrunched up tight against my body, my dick so hard and throbbing. My nipples had hardened too, and goosebumps erupted all over my flesh. I was about to take Heather's ass.

I pulled out of her hot pussy and slid upward, teasing the entrance to her back door.

"Thank you for this, Heather," I said. "Thank you for giving me this gift."

I breached her tight rim.

This time she did more than gasp. She yelled out.

"This is the toughest part, baby. Just breathe out. Let it feel good." I plunged in the rest of the way.

God, so tight, so warm, like a woolen glove for my cock. My instinct was to pull out and thrust back in, but I had to let her get used to the fullness first.

"You feel amazing, baby. So fucking good. You let me know when you're ready. I'll stay here until you are."

"I'm okay," she whimpered. "Show me what this is like, Jett. I want to feel this with you."

Pure emotion surged through me. I no longer wanted to be Jett. This wasn't happening to Jett. This was happening between Heather and Jeremy.

"Heather, baby." I closed my eyes and gritted my teeth to keep from exploding inside her tight ass. "Call me Jeremy. Please. It's my real name."

She lifted her head and twisted her neck to look back at me, her eyes wide.

"It's okay, baby. Please. Call me Jeremy."

And she smiled. A more radiant smile than I'd ever seen on her beautiful face. "Fuck my ass"—her eyes were heavy-lidded and sultry—"Jeremy."

CHAPTER TWENTY-SIX

HEATHER

Jeremy. Such a beautiful name. And right now my ass was full of this beautiful man's cock.

Such sweet fullness. Yes, it had hurt going in, but right now, I felt as close as I possibly could to this man—this man I had fallen in love with. This was a gift I could only give once. I'd squandered my original virginity on some stupid high school guy.

Now I had squandered my anal virginity to a rock star who would never love me.

But I loved him. Right now, that was all that mattered to me, as I relished the feeling of his hardness inside my most private place.

And though there could never be anything between us, he had given me a gift I'd always cherish. He'd given me his name.

"Are you sure, baby?" he asked.

"Yes, Jeremy. I'm sure."

He pulled out and thrust back into my ass.

Such a different sensation. Foreign and forbidden. And oh, so good.

Tears welled up in my eyes—tears of joy laced with

sadness. I was so happy to be sharing this part of me with a man I loved. I tried not to think of the fact that I would never have this again. As he continued to thrust in and out of my ass, the feeling of fullness morphed from exquisite pain to exquisite pleasure.

I fumbled underneath me, finding my clit. My pussy juices had dripped down, and my clit was slick. I began rubbing it ferociously, willing the orgasm that was rocking toward the precipice to gush forward.

"God, Jeremy!" I screamed against the pillow as my climax fractured me into a million pieces.

"Damn, Heather. I can't...hold...on— Ah!"

He plunged so deeply into me, I swore we became one being for a moment.

He fell on top of me, the sweat from his chest sticky against my back.

"God, baby," he whispered against my ear. "That was fucking spectacular."

Yes, it had been. For me, at least. Jett had no doubt experienced the rapture of anal sex many times before with many women. He'd probably been up Janet's ass, up Lindy's ass. Up myriad asses of myriad women.

Don't think that now, Heather. Just revel in what you experienced for the first time. Let yourself enjoy it.

"Yes," I replied. "It was."

Jett rolled over and lay on his back. I turned on my side to regard him. His hair was plastered against his neck and shoulders. His eyes were dark and heavy-lidded. His lips red and swollen from all our kissing.

I crawled into his arms without thinking.

He wrapped me close to him, kissing me on my forehead.

I didn't know what to say, so I didn't say anything. I just savored the feeling of our sated bodies and minds together in our afterglow.

♦ ♦ ♦ ♦

I must've fallen asleep because I opened my eyes to find myself in Jett's bed, but he was gone. The night sky shone through his window. Though the door to his bathroom was closed, I could hear the soft *whoosh* of the shower. I wanted to get up and join him, but I wasn't sure if that would be too presumptuous.

Of course, his cock had just been in my ass.

I sat up, ready to leave the bed and join him, when the water stopped. A minute later, he emerged from the bathroom, a black towel around his waist. He rubbed the wetness out of his long hair with another one.

"Hey," he said. "You're up."

"Yeah." I cleared my throat, my nerves skittering. "I should really be going."

"Are you kidding? I just showered so we could start again."

So we could start again? Of course he had to wash up. I was well aware of the personal hygiene required with anal sex. But why hadn't he asked me to join him?

He finished squeezing moisture out of his hair and threw the used towel into a hamper. "First, we should do some carboloading. I'll go down to the kitchen. My cook is off today, but she always leaves some awesome leftovers for me."

I opened my mouth to speak, but my stomach growled. I

hoped he hadn't heard it. It was the first indication I had that I was actually hungry. I hadn't eaten much of the dinner with Alicia Hopkins for obvious reasons.

He walked out of the room, still wearing nothing but a towel.

I was sweaty and messy. I had no idea how long he would be gone, but I figured it wouldn't hurt for me to step into the shower for a few minutes just to rinse off. I got up and walked into his decadent bathroom.

The warm water from all those showerheads felt like drops of nectar on my sweaty body. I shampooed my hair quickly and ran a soapy cloth over the essentials. But when I reached to turn off the faucet, a warm hand stopped me.

"Finished already?" Jett said.

"Yeah. What are you doing back in here? You already had a shower."

"I didn't have a shower with a beautiful woman, though."

I smiled shakily. "You could've woken me up."

"Believe me, baby, I thought about it. But you looked so angelic, with your hair fanned out on my pillow, your lips so red and perfect, that cute little snore—"

"Hey! I don't snore."

He laughed. "Of course you don't. Anyway, I didn't have the heart to wake you."

My heart surged. So he *had* wanted to shower with me.

Now was my chance. I would have loved to wash his hair, but he'd already done that. Instead, I slid against his body and wrapped my arms around him. We stood there, letting the hot water pelt us, just holding each other. The pressure of his lips on my head made my heart lurch once more. He'd kissed my forehead after we'd had sex, and now he kissed the top of my head. It wasn't a sexual kiss. If I hadn't known better, I'd have thought it was a kiss of love.

His cock hardened and pushed into my belly.

Not a kiss of love after all. Just lust on his part.

Nothing I didn't already know. I had to be okay with that. At least I'd been with him alone. I had come with Janet just for the chance to be with him once more, and I had gotten a lot more than I bargained for. For that, I was grateful.

Without saying a word, Jett lifted me in his strong arms and set me down upon his erection. Our bodies were wet and slick, and I wrapped my arms around his neck to stabilize myself as he pulled me on and off his cock.

My nipples hardened into tight knobs rubbing against his hard chest. They hadn't had any attention today other than from Janet. As great as her lips had felt, it had been purely physical pleasure. No emotions involved. With Jett, so many emotions hurtled through me—emotions that I had to be ready to say goodbye to when I eventually left his house today.

But I didn't have to say goodbye just yet. I grasped a handful of his wet hair and pulled, bringing his lips to mine. We kissed with a ferocity I had never known. All lips, teeth, and tongue—as ravenous as the way he was fucking me. As I slid against his slick body, my clit rubbed against his pubic hair, and soon I was tumbling into another vast climax.

I sobbed into him, still kissing him, my tongue probing every part of his mouth—his gumline, the inside of his cheeks, the roof of his mouth.

He set me down on his cock so forcefully I thought I might break in half, and I flowed straight into another orgasm. I felt every contraction as he spurted into me.

He continued to hold me as I broke the kiss and panted against his neck.

I choked back a tiny sob. No need to get emotional. We were still going to eat something together, and then maybe we would go back to his bed.

I would see to it that we did. If this was the only night I would have with Jett, I'd milk it for all it was worth.

CHAPTER TWENTY-SEVEN

JETT

It took all my strength to set Heather down and turn off the shower. I wrapped her in a plush bath towel and helped her dry her hair. Then I dried my own—again—and wrapped another towel around my waist. She looked so beautiful. No makeup on her peaches-and-cream complexion, her hair—the wetness brought out a darker shade of red—tumbling in damp spirals over her shoulders and back. And her eyes... When she looked at me...

I couldn't go there. What I saw in her eyes was also reflected back in my own.

She was falling in love with me.

The thought filled me with elation, pure joy.

And also devastation.

I couldn't drag her into this. I had other people to consider. I needed to create some distance, though I hated the thought.

I had already brought in some food. We could at least share a small snack. Then I would take her home.

I took her hand and led her to a table in the corner of my bedroom where I had set up some bread, cold cuts, and fruit, along with a bottle of Bordeaux.

"I was hoping for something a little more substantial, but this is all the cook left in my fridge. I hope you like sandwiches. I have peppered turkey and corned beef."

"Sounds perfect." She took a seat at the table.

I quickly opened the bottle of Bordeaux and poured us each a glass. "This is a great year. It can even class up corned beef sandwiches."

She laughed. It sounded like happy laughter, which filled my heart with joy. She was beautiful when she laughed. Of course, Heather Myles would be beautiful doing anything, wearing anything. She was especially beautiful wearing nothing.

She took a sip of wine. "That's really good. I don't know much about wine, but it's better than anything I've tasted before."

"I don't know much about wine either. My liquor store has a great sommelier, and I let him pick for me. He hasn't disappointed me yet." I smiled. "So what's your pleasure? Turkey or corned beef?"

"Both," she said. "I really didn't realize how hungry I was until now."

"Both it is." I piled meat on a sandwich for her. "Mustard? Mayo? Swiss cheese?"

"All of the above."

I placed her sandwich on a napkin, handed it to her, and then prepared one for myself.

"So," she said, her mouth full of sandwich, "I had no idea Jett wasn't your real name."

I let out a guffaw. "Who would be named Jett Draconis?"

"You mean Draconis isn't real, either?"

"God, no. My agent"—read Alicia—"liked it because it means dragon. She thought it sounded like a rock name."

"What's your real last name then?"

"Gustafson. It's Swedish."

"Jeremy Gustafson..." She took another bite, chewed, and swallowed. "You don't look Swedish."

"My dad was Swedish. My mom is German and Irish. My brother looks Swedish. He has blond hair and blue eyes." I saddened at the thought of my brother for a moment. He'd had a tough life, much tougher than I had now being stuck with Alicia's ultimatum.

He was the reason I had to let Heather go.

"I didn't know you had a brother."

"Yeah. He's two years older than I am." I frantically thought about ways to change the subject. "Do you have brothers or sisters?"

That ought to do it.

"Just me. The one and only."

She stopped talking then and concentrated on eating. Maybe she didn't want to talk about her family life any more than I did. At the moment, that was a good thing.

We gobbled up the rest of our sandwiches in silence.

Luckily, we still had more wine. I wasn't ready to say goodbye to Heather yet. Originally I had planned to feed her and then take her back to bed. My second thoughts had emerged when I realized she was feeling something more for me than I'd realized—something I could never return, though I wanted to more than anything in the world.

I topped off both of our wineglasses, and she took another sip.

"So remember when I asked you, the first night we met, whether you ever thought you were selling out by not pursuing opera?"

I nodded.

"I'm sorry I asked you that."

"Why? It was a valid question."

She took another sip of wine, her lips trembling just a bit. "Because first of all, it was none of my business. I had no right to judge you like that. You're hugely talented, and you've become an enormous success. You're using your God-given gifts."

"Everyone has to start somewhere." I smiled. "Bryan Cranston once did a commercial for hemorrhoid ointment."

That got a laugh out of her.

"Hey, he was acting."

"Yeah, he was. He did what he had to do to make it to the top, just like you have."

I was starting to get a little uncomfortable. I'd had a lot of help along the way, and I entered into a terrible agreement to get there—something I was rapidly seeing hadn't been worth it.

"I'm certainly no hero in that regard, Heather."

"But you kind of are. You're not doing opera. That doesn't mean you won't someday. Right now you're making enough money so that later, you *can* pursue opera. I always wanted to write for the big screen. I wasn't willing to settle for anything less. But where has that gotten me? Working my butt off as a waitress, getting my ass pinched—"

"What?" My ire rose. "You get your ass pinched?"

"This is LA, Jett. You know how it is here."

"You need to quit that job."

She arched one eyebrow. "I *need* that job. It's how I pay my bills."

"What if you no longer had to work? What if I..." I couldn't finish.

"What if you what? Paid my bills for me? In exchange for what? Sex?" She stood.

"Heather, no. That isn't what I was going to say." In truth, it had been exactly what I was going to say, minus the *payment in sex* part.

"Well... What then?"

I shook my head. "Never mind. But I will take care of anyone who pinches you from now on. You just let me know."

"I don't actually get all of their names, *Jett.*"

Jett. Coming from her lips, my name sounded as fake as it was. I wanted to be Jeremy to her. I wanted to be myself, not Jett Draconis, rock star extraordinaire.

"I don't like it, Heather."

"I'm not actually crazy about it myself, but the pinchers are at least usually good tippers. Besides, I'm seeing now that some of it is my fault."

"Are you crazy? None of this is your fault. No one has the right to touch you without your consent."

"Oh, no, I didn't mean it that way. What I mean is... I've been afraid of selling out. That if I didn't hold out for the big screen, I would be settling. But you've helped me see that that's not the case. I could be writing for TV, or digital entertainment. I could be writing webinars. I could be doing a lot that would flex my writing skills and also make me money. I've been kind of blind, I think."

"It's not a bad thing to *not* want to sell out." God, how I knew that. Though I enjoyed my life and the music I created, the devil's bargain I'd made with Alicia was quickly becoming the bane of my existence.

"I'm not saying it's bad. I just think I could be using the time I spend working at the diner doing some writing that would actually make money. That way I could at least be practicing my own form of art, just the way you are."

Her eyes sparkled as she looked at me with something extraordinary—almost veneration. I certainly didn't deserve that honor.

"I think it's amazing that you found a way to make money doing what you love."

"Honestly, baby, it's just as hard for rock stars to break into the scene as it is for opera singers. Maybe harder."

"But you did it, Jett. You did it, and you have this amazing career."

"But I might be ruining my voice for future endeavors."

She laughed at that. Actually laughed. "You already told me that you know how to keep your voice healthy."

"Yeah, you're right."

"Then why did you just say that?"

Why had I? Because I was damned uncomfortable with this conversation. I would still be a nobody in LA without Alicia Hopkins and the deal I'd struck with her.

That was something Heather Myles would *never* know about. She was as pure of soul as I'd come across since I moved to LA, and I didn't want to taint that.

And that was when I knew I would take her to bed again.

I had to be with her once more. First I'd see if she'd let me bind her, to show her how I liked to make love. Then, after that, I'd take her in the most basic position—her lying on her back, knees curled up, and me on top of her, driving my hard cock into her wet pussy while we gazed into each other's eyes.

I needed that last memory of this perfect woman.

CHAPTER TWENTY-EIGHT

HEATHER

He didn't answer my question about why he had said he might be ruining his voice for opera work. Instead he met my gaze, his eyes alight with flaming intensity.

He didn't speak. He simply rose, took the wineglass from my hand, set it on the table, and then pulled me out of my chair and into his arms. He laid me gently on his bed and released me from the towel covering my middle. He discarded his own towel as well and joined me on the bed.

I lay on my back, and he lay next to me on his side, supported on his shoulder, still gazing down at me with burning passion. He trailed his finger over my forehead, pushing my hair out of my eyes and then gliding it down my cheek and over my swollen lips.

"Jett—"

"Jeremy," he said, his voice a rasp.

"Jeremy, I love your touch." I fought the desire to tear up. This truly would be the last time we were together. I'd had more time with him than I'd ever dreamed of when Janet had suggested her scheme. It had turned out better than I ever expected.

But now it would be even harder to let go.

"I love your touch too, baby." He brushed his lips softly against my cheek.

He had kissed my forehead, the top of my head, and now my cheek. Those were a lover's kisses, not the lustful kisses of someone who just wanted to fuck.

Perhaps he felt as much as I did.

I forced that thought out of my head. I couldn't go there. Not when I knew it couldn't possibly be. He was just attracted to me. We had this intense physical thing on both of our parts. He was getting me out of his system, and I should be doing the same.

It wasn't working, though. The more time I spent with Jett—Jeremy—the more time I *wanted* to spend with him. He had already taught me so much about following my dreams. All this time, I could've been flexing my artistic muscles by doing something other than what my ultimate dream was.

"Jeremy, I need to tell you something."

"No, you don't."

Hmm. That was strange. "What do you mean?"

He hesitated for a moment. Then, "I don't mean anything. What do you want to tell me?"

"Well...you changed my life. Really."

He opened his mouth, but I placed two fingers over his lips.

"Let me finish. I'm not going to say anything to freak you out. I promise. What I mean is, you taught me that it's not selling out to take a different path to your dream. That's what I'm going to do. I'm going to give my two weeks' notice at the diner tomorrow."

Those last words actually surprised me. I hadn't made that decision until just that moment. But it was the right decision. I would find a way to make money from my writing. People were always looking for freelance writers and editors. I would find something, and I would make it work, while still holding on to my ultimate dream of writing for the big screen. Plus, I had the contact with Laney for the paranormal TV series. Sure, nothing could come of it, but maybe something would.

"You should know, Heather, that I *did* have help on my way up." His voice cracked a little, as though he was nervous.

"No one gets to the top on his own. I know that."

"But I had..." He paused a moment. "I don't want to talk about that now, not when I have a beautiful woman in my bed." Again he ran his finger down my cheek and this time down my neck, my shoulder, over the swell of my breasts, and to my nipple. "I want to make love to you, Heather."

Make love. That was just a euphemism for fucking, as far as he was concerned, but I liked the words nonetheless.

"Please, Jeremy," I said, a note of pleading in my voice. "Please make love to me."

He rolled on top of me, bracing his weight on his arms and legs, and lowered his lips to mine. He teased me at first, licking my lips, nibbling them. When I stuck my tongue out, hoping he would take the hint, he sucked on the tip of it for a moment and then went back to tiny kisses on my lips, cheeks, and neck.

My nipples hardened instantly, and I strained forward, aching for him to kiss me deeply.

But he seemed determined to go slowly. So I would savor

it. After all, this would be the last time with Jett Draconis.

The *only* time with Jeremy Gustafson.

I closed my eyes, forcing the tears not to form. Crying wouldn't let me savor this experience. I vowed to concentrate on what was happening now, to be in the moment. The tears could come later, when I would never see Jett again.

He was still raining tiny kisses all over my face. When his lips softly pressed against my closed eyelids, I let out a soft sigh.

Another thing no man had ever done to me. It was so sweetly sexy, so endearing yet such a turn-on at the same time.

When he had covered my face with kisses, he moved to my left earlobe and tugged on it. "My lips are going to touch every inch of your flesh, baby. Every fucking inch."

I exhaled softly. This would be torture. Blissful torture. I would be so ripe by the time he got to my pussy that I would be ready to fall off the vine.

His lips traveled over my forehead to my other ear, where he tugged on the lobe again and then ran his tongue over the outer edge, making me shiver. He darted his tongue inside, and a tickle landed between my legs. He thrust his tongue in and out of my ear, as if emulating what he would do to my pussy later.

I'd had no idea the inside of my ear was so sensitive. I squirmed beneath him, moaning, sighing, saying his name.

Jeremy. Jeremy. Jeremy.

When he was done torturing my ear, he slid his lips over my neck to my shoulder. Sweet Jesus, such sensitivity. He left goosebumps in his wake, repositioning himself on my side so he could kiss down my arm all the way to my hands and then my fingertips. He turned a hand over and planted several wet kisses against an area of my palm that was more sensitive than I had known. He kissed each finger, sucking the tips into his mouth as he went.

My body quaked on the bed. With my free hand, I reached across my body and stroked his forearm, relishing the muscle, the sinew, the warmth of his skin. I trailed my fingers over the lines of his Celtic lion tattoo. I had meant to ask him the story behind it, but I'd gotten sidetracked.

His stage name meant dragon. His surname was Swedish. But he had said his mother was German and Irish. Irish... Perhaps there was a story behind his tattoo, one that had to do with his heritage.

But then those thoughts fled my head as he kissed up my arm again, over my chest, and took one hard nipple between his lips. He sucked and tugged, and I squirmed beneath him, wanting more, needing more.

When he dropped my nipple, I whimpered.

"I want to continue kissing you all over, Heather," he said, his voice low and husky. "But I want to tie you down. I want to tie your wrists and ankles to my bed. Do you trust me? May I do that?"

My heartbeat surged. He wanted to...

"What?" The words left my lips and seemed to echo throughout the room.

"It will be good for you, baby. I promise. But if you're uncomfortable, I'll just keep kissing you the way I am, moving my lips up and down your hot body, tasting every part of you that you have to offer me."

"What?" I said again.

"Have you ever been bound before? Bound for your own pleasure?"

I bit my lip and shook my head.

"I know I have no right to ask this of you," he said. "I'm asking anyway. I'm asking because it will be amazing for you, and I want you to remember this night. I want it imprinted on your memory so that you'll never be able to forget what we shared together."

I would never forget it anyway. I didn't need some extrasensory device to make me remember this. But maybe he thought I did. Maybe he really thought this would make it better for me.

The idea of being bound frightened me...but also intrigued me. Intrigued me to the point that the throbbing between my legs intensified.

Could I trust this man? I hardly knew him, yet in a way I felt like we were old souls who had known each other for millennia. Not that I believed in that bullshit, and in my head, I knew we would never be together long-term.

Agreeing to this didn't make any sense. Just as agreeing to the little show with Janet hadn't made any sense. I'd agreed to it anyway.

So I wasn't completely surprised when I said, "All right, Jeremy. I trust you."

CHAPTER TWENTY-NINE

JETT

I closed my eyes for a moment and thanked the universe for this gift. The thought of Heather Myles tied down, legs spread, ready for whatever I was going to give her filled me with joy.

This would be a night neither of us would soon forget. I certainly wouldn't. I would never forget the fan of her auburn hair across the dark blue of my pillow. I would never forget the softness of her flesh beneath my lips. I would never forget her soft moans as I pleasured her. I would never forget the amazing talks we had shared, the laughs.

My eyes still closed, I imprinted all of it on my memory, even knowing it wasn't necessary.

I would *never* forget.

I opened my eyes. "Are you sure, baby?"

Her amber eyes glowed. "I'm sure."

My cock was hard, and when I stood, it jutted straight out, straining toward Heather. But that would wait. I'd show her the ecstasy that binding could bring her. I walked to my chest of drawers and pulled out the leather bindings that had been perfectly made to fit the dimensions of my head and footboards.

I had used these bindings many times, with Janet, Lindy, many others. I forced that thought from my mind. Right now, these were new bindings, had never been used.

They had been made for today. For Heather.

Heather's skin paled, and I could tell she was apprehensive. Clearly she had never done anything like this before, and her trust touched me.

"Are you sure?" I asked again.

"Yes."

"Reach your hands over your head."

She complied, and I quickly found each wrist, adjusting the length of the straps.

"Now spread your legs, baby."

Again, she complied, and I bound her to the posts.

Then I stood at the foot of the bed, simply staring at her. A gourmet feast not just for my eyes and my tongue, but for every part of me.

For my heart.

I couldn't go there. As much as I wanted to, it just wasn't possible.

But I would give us both something so indelible that it would be a mark on our souls forever.

I walked to the side of the bed and sat down, cradling my fingers over the swell of her breasts, her nipples.

And then I began to kiss her.

I began at her neck and her shoulder, the arm I hadn't yet kissed that was now bound. I trailed my lips over her soft flesh, kissing, licking, twirling my tongue in figure eights over her smooth skin. So, so sweet. So, so good. She shuddered beneath my touch, goosebumps erupting, soft sighs escaping her throat. I inhaled her scent, raspberries and cream, her flavor salty in comparison to the sweet shine of perspiration. The aroma of her pussy rose in the air—apples, musk, Heather.

Heather Myles was a feast for all my senses. My nose drew in the sweet scents that were uniquely hers. My eyes roved over that beautiful body—her heavy-lidded eyes, her swollen red lips, her plump breasts and hard pink nipples, her flat belly, the trimmed red hair between her legs, and the swell of her clit. My mouth tasted the silkiness of her skin, the sweetness of her mouth, the tanginess of her pussy. My ears adored the soft sighs from her throat, the moans, the groans. When she said my name.

Jeremy. Jeremy. Jeremy.

So sweet the sound of my given name from her lips.

And the sense of touch. My fingers, calloused from guitar playing, roamed over every inch of her. She was soft where I was hard, lighter where I was darker. She was perfect—the perfect woman in every way.

I sucked the tip of her index finger into my mouth, and that beautiful sigh met my ears once more as she tugged at the bindings.

"It feels so good. Want..."

"What, baby?"

"Want to...touch you."

I smiled against the pale skin of her forearm. "That's what makes it so good. You want...but can't have."

"Not fair. You get to touch me."

I chuckled. "When I suggested this little game, baby, I

never claimed it would be fair."

She closed her eyes, groaning. "I won't survive this."

"But you will."

"I've a mind to tie you up when we're done. Make you endure this torture."

I chuckled again. No woman had ever tied me up. I was anything but submissive. But for Heather Myles? I might just allow it.

I trailed my lips down her arm again and then to her chest, where I began teasing her other nipple.

Some women liked their breasts slapped. I was usually happy to oblige. But not Heather. Her breasts were works of art. She was too precious to me to slap.

Boy, did that thought have a lot of connotation. Which is why I erased it from my head and concentrated on the beautiful nipple. Her areola tightened up and was textured under my tongue. My dick was so hard. I was tempted to just shove myself into her and fuck her into oblivion.

But still I worked on her nipple, my fingers finding the other one and pinching. She moaned softly, her hips undulating. And I couldn't help myself. My hand drifted from her nipple across her soft belly, my fingers entwining through her curls and then dipping into her hot pussy.

And finding heaven.

She was soaking wet.

Again, my cock begged me to plunge into nirvana.

But I held myself in check, letting her nipples slip from my mouth and then spreading tiny kisses over the flatness of her abdomen. On every part of her body, the surface of her skin was slightly different. Soft, sweet, still a bit salty, but different textures under my lips and tongue.

I was so close to her wet heat, and the aroma was driving me slowly insane. My cock was granite and stationary between my legs, so hard it was immobile. I buried my nose in her vulva and inhaled. Then, though it pained me, I skipped over her pussy and placed sucking kisses on her inner thighs.

"You have *got* to be kidding me," came her sultry voice from the head of the bed.

I smiled against her thighs, wet from her juices, as I lapped at them.

I moved to the top of her knee and then down her calf. When I got to her bound ankle, I massaged it a bit, just in case the bindings were a little rough on her, and then slid my tongue over her instep.

Even her feet were gorgeous, her toenails painted a light, frosty pink. I kissed and lightly sucked on each toe, and then worked my way back up her leg. I inhaled her vulva again— God I was so fucking hard—and then, avoiding her pussy once more—fucking hardest thing I've ever done—I slid my lips and hands down her other shapely leg.

She moaned again, whimpering.

I had kissed almost every part of her at this point. But I was so far from done.

After massaging her other leg, ankle, and foot, kissing each toe, I traveled back up, inhaling once more the fumes from her sweet cunt and then sliding up to take her other nipple between my lips. I bit it gently, eliciting more whimpers from her.

Then, though my original plan had been to unbind her,

turn her over, and kiss the rest of her, I could wait no longer. I straddled her and shoved my hard-as-rock cock deep into her succulent heat.

Sweet heaven. I had never been this hard in my life, and I felt every ridge, every tuck inside her. She cloaked me perfectly, teased me, sucked me into her body.

This.

This was the essence of life.

I had found a soul mate in Heather Myles.

A soul mate that would be denied me.

But damn it, I would make love to her this one time.

I had already fucked her, had already taken her ass.

What I was doing to her now was nothing new, but it was different. It transcended everything else in my life.

She writhed beneath me as I brought her to one orgasm and another.

Though it pained me, I withdrew for a moment and swiftly unbound her. Then I sank back into her, and she curled her arms and legs around me.

This was what I'd imagined. Lovemaking in its purest form.

And when my balls bunched up, and the tiny convulsions started at the base of my cock, I opened my mouth and let flow the words I'd been holding close to my heart for what seemed like forever.

"Goddamnit, Heather. I fucking love you."

CHAPTER THIRTY

HEATHER

I was flying. Soaring out over the vast blue of the Pacific Ocean. When I inhaled, I could even smell the glorious scent of the beach. Seagulls cawing, surfers shouting, children laughing... and in the midst of the beauty of the chaos,

I fucking love you.

I flew into another orgasm.

The words were nothing but fantasy. They hadn't come from Jett. I knew that.

Though I longed to say the same words to the man pumping above me, I couldn't force them from my throat. Instead, low moans, soft cries emerged as my climax entwined itself around my very soul.

I wrapped my arms around his neck and pulled him toward me.

The kiss was deep and passionate. I gave him everything I had with that kiss. Everything in my heart and soul, knowing it was the last time.

I reached toward him with every cell in my body, every emotion in my heart.

I love you, Jeremy, I said with that kiss. *For the rest of my*

life, I will love no other as I love you.

Even though his head couldn't hear my words, his heart and soul could. I was sure of it.

I cried out at the loss when he broke the kiss.

He lay down on his back, pulling me into his arms. His kisses became softer. Not as deep, not as ferocious.

But they lasted a long, long time.

♦ ♦ ♦ ♦

When I woke up, I was still in Jett's bed, still naked, with him spooned against my back. His breaths were deep and regular as they drifted into my hair.

I was thirsty, so I edged away from him, got up, and headed to the bathroom for a glass of water. Then I went back to the bed and stood next to it, staring down at the beautiful man—the man I'd been closer to than anyone in my life just over a period of a few days. I had learned so much from him. And I knew what I could do to repay him.

I could leave.

I wouldn't be the needy woman who had inadvertently fallen in love with the rock star whose life had no room for a real relationship. I had to think about these few days as he did—a fun time, but nothing more. If he'd truly rigged the bomb threat at the concert to save me so I'd sleep with him, we'd both gotten what we wanted.

It wasn't his fault that I wanted more, would always want more.

My heart lurched, but I sniffed back the tears that threatened to fall.

I crept slowly through the room, gathered my clothes, and went back to the bathroom to get dressed. I would've liked a shower, but I didn't want to take the chance of waking Jett.

I sneaked out of his room, down the stairs, and out the door.

♦ ♦ ♦ ♦

I awoke to my ringtone blaring.

"Hello?" I said into the phone.

"Where the hell are you?"

Jett's voice. I took the phone from my ear and checked the time. Early morning. Six thirty a.m.

"I'm at home."

"I woke up and you were gone."

"I... I'm sorry. I thought it would be better if—"

"*You* thought? What about what *I* think?"

Jett had been so sweet to me. Rough but gentle. The man was the ultimate paradox—like he was being tugged two different ways.

And in truth, he was. Part Jett, part Jeremy.

But he had to be Jett. Jett was the success.

"What *do* you think, J— Jett?" I'd been about to say Jeremy, but caught myself.

"I... I don't know. I don't ever fucking know what I think. Someone else has to think for me."

"What are you talking about?"

"I'm talking about... The fact that I invited a woman to my bed, and I wake up in the morning and she's fucking gone. Don't I mean just a little bit more to you than that?"

"You mean a lot to me. But you're Jett Draconis. I'm just a nobody. You've had a lot of women in your bed. Do you call them all in the morning demanding to know where they went?"

"Goddamnit!"

"Is that your answer?"

"No, that's not my fucking answer. I got another call. I'm sorry. I have to take it."

I let out a breath I had been holding. "I understand."

The call dropped.

Apparently, someone else was more important than knowing why I had left his bed.

Though I wasn't surprised, sadness swelled within me. I put my phone down and then curled up in a fetal position in my bed.

Sleep did not return.

CHAPTER THIRTY-ONE

JETT

I truly meant nothing to her. She had ignored my confession of love, which my head knew was just as well. The words should never have left my lips. She and I could never be, a fact that was hammered back into me by the call that had interrupted us.

"Hey, Mom," I said.

"Thank God you answered, Jeremy." My mother's voice was breathy with panic.

"What's going on?"

"Ty got an anonymous phone call early this morning. It was pretty ominous. Just said they had evidence that his alibi was fake. That you hadn't been with him that night."

Anger descended upon me like an avalanche. Fucking Alicia Hopkins. I'd take care of that bitch. "It was probably just a prank, Mom. I wouldn't worry about it." But my words were empty. Already my heart was thundering. Alicia was marking her territory. She knew I was feeling something more for Heather, something I wasn't allowed to feel.

Why had I jumped off that stage?

The bomb threat had turned out to be nothing. Heather

would have been fine.

But I hadn't known that at the time. All I'd known was that I had to keep her safe. I *had* to.

I'd never told my mom and brother about Alicia's threats and the deal I'd made with her. I'd basically prostituted myself for fame and fortune. For success.

That was the real reason I could never be with Heather.

Even if I could somehow get out of the whole Alicia thing, Heather deserved so much better than a man who would sell his soul for fame and fortune.

"Can you come to Chicago?" my mother asked.

"I can't, Mom. I've got rehearsal every day and concerts nearly every night. And our Glass Houses tour starts in less than a month. There's just no time."

"I know. I understand. There's never any time."

"Mom..."

"It's not that we don't appreciate everything you do for us, Jeremy. It's just that sometimes..." She sighed. "Sometimes I wonder if it was worth the cost."

Hell, I'd wondered that myself more than once. Way more than once since I'd met Heather.

But my mother wasn't talking about my deal with Alicia. She didn't know about that.

"What do you mean?" I asked.

"We never see you anymore. We miss you, Jeremy."

"Mom, your house is paid off. You have everything you could possibly want." I'd already made sure my mom and brother would be taken care of in high style for the rest of their lives.

"Not everything," she said. "We don't have *you*."

♦ ♦ ♦ ♦

I banged on Alicia's door.

"Where is she?" I demanded when her maid answered.

"I'm sorry, but she can't be disturbed right now. She's with her masseur."

"Really? I know what that means." I stepped inside Alicia's mansion.

"Mr. Draconis, I can't let you—"

I whisked past her and ran up the stairs and down the hallway to the door of her dungeon. I opened it and walked in, expecting to find her tied up and getting pounded.

I was surprised to find the room empty. Maybe she truly was having a massage.

I stormed into each room and finally found her, just as her maid had said, facedown on a massage table with a muscular blond man fondling her uncovered glutes.

Yeah, professional. I was pretty sure his finger would be sliding up her hole at any moment.

He looked up at me and said in a low, soft voice, "We're in the middle of a session, sir. We need privacy. Thank you for understanding."

"Sorry, dickhead. I need a word with your mistress there."

"She's not my—"

Alicia's head popped up from the table, her neck turning toward me. "Jett, what are you doing here?"

My name got the masseur's attention. "Holy shit! You're Jett Draconis! I'm a huge fan."

"Thanks. Nice to meet you." I turned back to Alicia. "We have business to discuss," I said through clenched teeth.

"Can it wait, darling? I'm so stressed out, and Anders is working out the kinks for me."

"You'll never be able to work out all the kink in her," I said to Mr. Muscles. "Trust me on that one." I walked forward. "You're done here, Anders."

"He is most certainly not done," Alicia said.

"What will it take? Money?" I said to Anders.

"Jett, really. You know I can buy and sell you a hundred times over. Whatever you offer him, I can offer more."

I turned to Anders. "How about a couple of front row tickets to the Emerald Phoenix concert next Friday?"

That got Anders's attention. "Really?"

"Get the fuck out of here right now and it's done, buddy," I said.

"Anders, don't listen to him. I can give you whatever tickets you want."

"But she can't get you tickets to a sold-out concert," I said. "*I* can."

Anders gently covered Alicia's derrière with a white towel. "Sorry, ma'am, but my husband loves Emerald Phoenix. In fact, he'd cream his pants if he knew I just met Jett Draconis."

"You have a card on you?" I asked.

Anders reached into his pocket, retrieved a business card, and handed it to me.

"Thanks. I'll have the tickets emailed to you."

A huge grin split Anders's chiseled cheeks. "Awesome." He grabbed my hand in both of his and shook it hard. "This is amazing. Thank you so much." He left the room.

I turned back to Alicia. "You leave my mother and brother alone."

"Why did you chase Anders away? Now I have to find another masseur, and I don't think I'll be able to find another one with such a nice cock."

"You're fucking him?" Not that I was surprised. "He's married. And gay."

"Money talks, Jett. You of all people should know that. I slip him a little Viagra, and he has no problem getting hard for me. He's so huge. He nearly splits my ass in two." She grinned.

I berated myself inwardly. I had let her get me off track. "You've been in contact with my mother. That needs to stop."

"It will stop when *you* stop seeing that little slut Heather Myles."

"Our deal was that I could fuck whoever I wanted to. I wanted to fuck Heather. Now I'm done." And I truly was. Since she'd ignored my confession of love in the heat of the moment, she clearly did not share my feelings. I had been mistaken when I thought I saw more in her eyes.

"You must think I'm some kind of idiot. You want much more than a fuck from Heather Myles. You've had her a couple times already now, and let me guess. You want her again, don't you?"

I didn't bother denying it. "Christ, Alicia, what I want has never been a part of our deal."

"You're mine."

"What's so special about me? Why do you need me at your fucking beck and call? You have Anders's big dick. If his dick matches those muscles of his, I'm sure as hell no competition for him."

"Correction. I *had* Anders's big dick. No longer."

"Why not? Offer him money, and he'll come back."

"Never. He left me in the middle of a session without even having the decency to give me a fuck first. He left for a few stupid concert tickets. I'll never hire him for anything again."

Well, then, Anders, I just did you a huge favor, whether you realize it or not. Concert tickets and your freedom in one afternoon. Now if I could only figure out how to do that for myself.

"Why me, Alicia?"

"What do you mean?"

"You know exactly what I mean. You can buy anyone you want. What's so special about me? Why do you insist that I be around to fuck you at your will? Why is it so important to you that I never fall in love? So important that you've blackmailed me with my family's freedom?"

No response, but her lips trembled slightly.

"Why, Alicia?" I demanded again. "Why do you torment me like this?"

"Because"—she slid her tongue over her lips like an asp getting ready to strike—"I *can*."

CHAPTER THIRTY-TWO

HEATHER

Susie pounced on my bed at ten a.m. I hadn't slept, but I'd lain in bed dreaming of my time with Jett and ruminating on his odd phone call earlier.

"Tell me *everything*," she demanded.

I so wasn't in the mood to recount the entire episode with Janet and then Jett in detail, and that was what she would want.

"Suze, I didn't sleep well. Why don't you ask Janet? She can fill you in."

Susie giggled. "I've already talked to her. She said you wouldn't do anything until Jett got there, and then all she did was go down on you and suck on your titties a little before Jett asked her to leave so you two could be alone."

I sighed. I should have known Susie would get the scoop any way she could.

"So how was it?" she asked again. "Did you like being with a girl?"

Had I? That part of it seemed like a blur now. Everything was Jett, Jett, Jett. My last time with Jett.

"It was okay."

"Okay? Jan's gorgeous!"

"Yeah, she is. But..."

"But what?"

"But...I'm not really into girls, I guess."

Frankly, I wasn't into guys anymore, either. I was into *one* guy.

One guy I'd never have again.

I was hopelessly in love with Jett Draconis. Or Jeremy Gustafson.

Which one was it?

It was both of them. It was the artistry and beauty of Jett Draconis. It was the gentility, sweetness, and raw talent of Jeremy Gustafson. It was the tenacity and devotion to music of both of them. They'd figured out how to use their God-given talents to get to the top.

And thinking of them as two different people was more than a little disturbing.

"You don't have any response to that?" Susie was saying.

Had she said something? "I'm sorry. What?"

"Jan said you're a great kisser. Better than most girls. You use more tongue."

"Oh?" I was oddly flattered. "I just kissed the way I always do."

"You don't have a lot of experience with girls. Bisexual girls, I mean. Men like to use a lot of tongue, so girls are used to keeping their tongues in their own mouths. The problem is, when a girl kisses another girl, neither of them lets their tongues stray out of their mouth. So what you get is basically a tongueless kiss. Since you'd never been with a girl before, that's what Jan was expecting from you. She said she was pleasantly surprised."

T.M.I.

I opened my mouth to respond to Susie, but I had no idea what to say.

Just as well, because Susie babbled on about kissing. I stopped listening after a while.

"So you want to go out and get some breakfast or something?"

I yawned. "Yeah, okay. Let me take a shower. I don't work till five. By the way, I'm giving my notice tonight."

Her eyes widened. "Really? Did you sell something?"

"Unfortunately, no. I do have a lead with that paranormal TV show, though. We'll see what happens. But I'm bound and determined to put my writing to good use. I'll write for bloggers. I'll write for e-zines. Heck, I'll write advertising for flyers. I spend way too much time on my feet in that diner making so-called contacts that don't lead to anything. Letting assholes pinch my ass."

"Jesus, Heather, where did this come from? You were always about paying the bills. About having something steady. About not pimping out your talents to write for tabloid crap."

"I just want to do what I love. I want to write. It doesn't really matter *what* I write, does it?"

"Well, it never mattered to me," she said. "But I was pretty darn sure it mattered to you. 'It's the big screen or nothing.' Those are the words of Heather Myles, I believe."

"Yeah... I'm kind of seeing things from a different angle now."

"Why?"

Why lie to her? "Honestly? Jett."

"Jett? What did he do?"

"Did you know his background is in opera?"

"No, I didn't."

"He went to graduate school at Northwestern with his keyboardist, Zane Michaels. Did you know he's a classical pianist?"

"No shit? Pretty boy Zane? Who gets more pussy than the rest of the band combined?"

"I know. I can't see it either, but he's amazing on the keyboard, so I bet he's even more amazing on a nine-foot grand."

"I can't see either of them in a tux," she said.

Oh, but I could. An image popped into my mind. Jett in a tux. A sleek black tuxedo covering his muscular body. A plain white shirt, no pleats or ruffles, with black button covers and suspenders. No cummerbund. Suspenders were classier. A white silk bow tie. And his gorgeous dark hair pulled back in a neat ponytail. Or maybe a messy man bun.

No. The ponytail for a tux.

"I'll just take a quick shower," I said again.

A quick *cold* shower.

CHAPTER THIRTY-THREE

JETT

In the late afternoon, I got out of a cab and walked toward my mother's house in Evanston, Illinois. The house was a restored 1920s mansion in an affluent area. I'd bought it for my mother when Emerald Phoenix earned its first gold record. My older brother, Tyler, had lived there with her for a while, but now he had his own place, also subsidized by me. He did carpentry work. He was an artist in his own right. He made gorgeous unique pieces that sold for top dollar.

He was finally happy. Finally moving forward with his life.

What I was about to do might destroy that.

I'd chartered a plane when I left Alicia's. She'd given me no choice. *Because I can.* I'd always known she was a bitch of the highest order who loved controlling people, but when she uttered those words, her eyes narrow yet shining with happiness, I knew the whole truth.

She was psycho.

I'd never really believed her when she said she would take me and my family down. Why would she? She had made me. Had made Emerald Phoenix into the sensation it was. Why would she ruin that? What purpose would it serve?

Now I knew it didn't matter whether a true purpose existed. She didn't care. She was nuts, and she'd do it for fun.

I rued the day I'd ever set eyes on the narcissistic, psycho bitch.

Zane and I had talent. We could have made it on our own, but we hadn't had the slightest idea how to become rock stars.

Alicia had created us.

I inhaled deeply and knocked on my mother's door.

A few minutes later, she opened it, her eyes sparkling with happiness when she saw me. "Jeremy! You said you couldn't come."

"I changed my mind." I entered as she held the door open for me. "Is Ty here by any chance?"

"Actually, he is. He came by with a new bookshelf for me. He's setting it up in the den. It's beautiful. Come see it. Ty!" she yelled. "Jeremy's home!"

My big brother, who could have been my twin except for his blond hair and blue eyes, sauntered in and gave me a bear hug. "Hey, Jer. What's the occasion?"

Tyler looked so happy. He had come such a long way with the best counseling my money could buy. I hated what I was about to do to him and my mother.

But I could no longer afford to keep the secret I'd been hiding for five years. Alicia was a ticking time bomb. I needed to take prophylactic measures.

"I need to talk to both of you," I said.

"Jeremy?" My mother touched my forearm. "What's the matter? Oh, no... That phone call I got... This has to do with that, doesn't it?"

I nodded solemnly. "I'm afraid it does."

"What phone call?" Tyler asked.

"Oh, Ty, I didn't want to bother you with this."

"Mom, you're not a bother. What is she talking about, Jeremy?"

"Tell him about the phone call, Mom," I said.

"It was nothing really, Ty. Just a prank call, I'm sure."

"Tell him," I said again.

"An anonymous call. Kind of a low female voice. She just said that she knew that Jeremy had given you a fake alibi."

Tyler threaded his fingers through his long blond hair. "Shit."

"You told me you didn't think it was anything to worry about, Jeremy," my mother said.

"Yeah, I did. At the time, I didn't think it was."

"And you changed your mind?" My mother's face turned pale.

"I'm not sure. It could still be nothing. But there's something I need to tell you guys. Something you have the right to know."

"You're not in any trouble, are you?" my mother said.

I raked my fingers through my hair, which was no doubt in complete disarray after the plane ride here. "Mom, we've all been in trouble since we made the decision we did seven years ago. The minute we decided I would be Tyler's alibi, we knew there was always a chance it could come back and bite us in the ass."

Tyler said nothing. Just stood, his body stiffening until he was as stationary as one of the exquisite tables he turned out from his shop.

My mother's lips trembled. "But it's been seven years, Jeremy. Seven years! What could possibly go wrong now?"

Alicia Hopkins. That was what could go wrong now.

"Can we sit down?" I asked.

Tyler was standing still, as if in a daze.

My mother went to him and touched his arm lightly. "Let's go sit down in the kitchen, Ty."

I followed my mother and my brother, my body numb, into the kitchen where I took a seat at her oak table. A beautiful piece that Tyler had specially crafted for her.

"Now tell us," my mother said. "What is this all about, Jeremy?"

CHAPTER THIRTY-FOUR

HEATHER

I knocked on the door to my manager's office.

"Yeah, come on in."

Knox Jacobson sat behind his desk, looking as slimy as usual, balding with a bad comb-over. He hit on most of his waitresses, including me. I'd been able to keep him at arm's length by spouting off some legal jargon that scared the hell out of him. My knowledge hadn't seemed to help the other girls, though. I still heard stories of what went on in his office behind closed doors.

He looked up. "What is it, Heather?"

"I need to give you my two weeks' notice, Knox. I'm going to be leaving the diner."

"May I ask why?"

It was none of his damned business. "I just want to focus more on my writing career. That's all."

"Oh? Did you sell?"

Why the hell did everyone ask me that? And what business was it of his anyway? "As a matter of fact, yes, I did sell something."

"Really? Congratulations. What studio bought one of

your scripts?"

Shit. Why had I lied? "I'm not at liberty to say just yet. Contract terms are still being negotiated." There. That sounded good.

"I see." He stood and walked around to me, holding out his hand. "I certainly wish you the best of luck."

As distasteful as it was, I took his sweaty hand. "I appreciate the opportunity you've given me here, Knox."

I turned to walk out of the office, when his hand came down on my ass.

I turned back, livid. "What the hell was that?"

"Just a little congratulatory pat. I didn't mean anything by it, Heather."

Such a swine! I walked backward to the door this time and left. Two weeks could not go by fast enough.

♦ ♦ ♦ ♦

Susie, with Janet and Lindy in tow, came by at midnight when my shift was over.

"We're on our way to a party at Zane Michaels's house," Lindy said. "And you're coming with us."

"I can't, you guys. I'm dead on my feet." No truer words. It had been an especially challenging shift. At least I had a pocket full of big tips to show for it.

"Oh, come on, girlfriend," Lindy said. "Jan says you're a great partier."

I looked at Janet, and she smiled a teasing smile.

"The four of us could put on quite a show for Zane. And you *know* Jett will be there." She winked.

Another reason I could not go to the party. I couldn't see Jett again. I especially couldn't see him showing interest in some other woman. After all, he'd had his fill of me. He'd staged a bomb threat just to be with me so he could get me out of his system.

I ought to be good and out of his system by now. After last night, nothing was left for us to do together.

"I really can't," I said again. "I'm exhausted, and I work the noon shift tomorrow."

"So you didn't give your notice?" Susie said.

"Oh, no. I did."

"Then who gives a shit about the noon shift tomorrow? Show up late. Show up drunk. What does it matter?"

"It's still my job, Suze. I still take it seriously."

As much as I loved Susie, she had a lot of growing up to do. But as long as she got her jollies partying and fucking rock stars, that wasn't going to happen anytime soon.

"Sometimes you're such a downer, Heather. We'll be sure to tell Jett you said hi." Susie turned.

"Now wait a minute, Suze," Janet said. "I think you're giving up too easily. And so are you, Heather. Let me tell you something. I've known Jett Draconis for a long time. Yeah, I've fucked him. Lindy has fucked him. Suze, you haven't, but you haven't been in this scene as long as we have. I've seen him with other women, with two, three, four at a time."

Was this supposed to make me feel better?

She continued, "But what I saw last night? I'd never seen *that* before."

"What do you mean?" Susie asked.

"Jett was possessive," Janet said. "Possessive like I had never seen him. He damn near threw me off your pussy, girlfriend. And then he didn't want anything to do with me."

"So?" I said.

"I just told you. I've seen him with two and three and four women at a time. And he always gives equal attention to all of them."

"What exactly are you saying?"

"I'm saying, Heather, that Jett is feeling something *more* for you. Something he has never felt for any woman that I've seen. Is it love? I have no idea. But it's something. And if you're feeling something more for him, you need to go to this party tonight."

"You're mistaken," I said. "I know what Jett is about. He sets his sights on a woman and pursues her until he gets her into bed. Then he's done. That's all he did with me. He just had to work a little harder. By staging the bomb threat so he could 'save' me."

"Girl, who told you that?" Lindy said.

"A friend of his. Alicia Hopkins."

"That bitch?" Janet shook her head. "She's lying to you. Jett would never stage a fake bomb threat at one of his concerts. That's not who he is. He adores his fans, and he would never interrupt a concert they paid good money for just to get a woman into bed."

My heart thundered. "You mean he jumped off the stage because he really thought he was saving me?" A lump formed in my throat and my skin grew warm.

"Of course he did," Lindy said. "Jett may like to fuck a lot of women and engage in orgies, but one thing anyone who knows him will tell you is that at heart, he's a good guy. A decent guy."

A smile tugged at the corner of my lips. Could Jett really be feeling something more for me? I was head over heels in love with him. Obviously, he wasn't there yet, but what if he could *get* there?

What if I could actually have a future with him?

I couldn't hold back my smile any longer. "Ladies, let's go to that party."

CHAPTER THIRTY-FIVE

JETT

Seven years earlier...

My brother's eyes were feral, and blood stained his hands. He stood, immobile, staring at me as if he were looking through me.

"Fuck, Ty. What have you done?"

"I didn't mean it, Jer. I meant to go over and scare him a little. I never thought..."

"Who? What?"

"That rapist Harley Massey. The police let him go. They fucking let him go!"

"Slow down, bro. What do you mean they let him go?"

"Not enough evidence. No probable cause to make an arrest. He can just rape my girlfriend, cause her suicide, and not even get a slap on the wrist. What the hell is wrong with our society, man?"

"Ty, it's Renee's word against his."

He advanced toward me. "You calling Renee a liar?"

I held up my hand, stopping him. "No. Of course not."

"Doesn't matter anyway. He admitted it to me. Said she had a hot little cunt. Goddamnit!" Tyler's fist landed on the oak desk he'd made for me.

"He could be lying. Just trying to bait you."

"He baited me, all right."

My neck prickled. My brother was manic right now. More manic than I'd seen him in a long time. "Where's your piece, Ty?"

"It's in the car."

"Man. All right. You stay here."

I hurried out to my brother's car and grabbed the gun from the passenger seat. It was cold, thank God. I breathed in relief as I brought it in.

"You didn't use the gun. That's good."

"Never took it in."

"Good. That's good, man. But you've got"—I gulped—"blood on your hands."

"It's my own. The fucker bit me."

Thank God! More relief surged through me. "You can press charges. Assault charges."

"But I went to his place."

"So? Did he let you in?"

"Yeah. So?"

"Then he had no right to attack you. I'm calling the cops."

Tyler walked toward me and grabbed the cell phone from my hands, throwing it across the room. "You can't."

"Why the hell not?"

"Harley's dead."

♦ ♦ ♦ ♦

Images came crashing back. Forcing my brother into the

shower. Then him crying in my arms as he described how he'd strangled Harley Massey with his bare hands. Then my interrogation.

Was Harley alone? Did anyone see you go into his place? Did anyone see you leave?

Yes.

No.

No. I don't think so.

He was going to get away with it. With raping Renee. With causing her death. I couldn't let it happen, Jer. I just couldn't.

Mom had come home soon after, and the two of us devised a plan.

I'd been home alone all evening. That much was true. What *wasn't* true was that Tyler had been with me.

But he was my big brother. A good guy, if a little impulsive. He was prone to manic attacks, so I made a deal with him and my mother.

Harley Massey was a scumbag with a drug and domestic violence record. No one would miss him. My brother was a mentally ill man but a creative genius. I'd give Tyler an alibi, and in exchange, he'd go into therapy for as long as it took to get his head on straight. Mom agreed to keep our secret.

My brother was as good as his word. With therapy and medication, his erratic behavior ceased, and he began to make something of himself. He grieved Renee, and he healed. After a year and a half, with him and Mom taken care of, I left for LA.

Zane and I had considered LA before, but I'd always begged out at the last minute. After the turmoil at home, though, and with Mom and Tyler doing well, I finally told Zane yes.

I needed a change.

So we went to LA.

And at a party, I met Alicia Hopkins.

The woman who created Jett Draconis and Zane Michaels.

The woman who held the fate of my family in her hands.

And now I had to tell them the truth.

"What is all this about, Jeremy?" my mother asked again.

"That anonymous call you got, Mom. It was a threat. Just not for you or Tyler. It was a threat for me."

"What are you talking about?"

I sank my head into my hands, fighting back tears. How could I tell them I'd prostituted myself for fame and fortune? Made a deal with the devil to rise to the top, and if I reneged, we'd all go down?

"Hey, man," Ty said. "Whatever it is, we'll get through it. We've been through worse, God knows."

My brother was intelligent, but he had no idea what deep shit we were all in. Tyler could be tried for murder, and Mom and I could be tried as accessories after the fact.

What a fucking mess.

Still, I couldn't bring myself to regret saving my brother that day. I regarded him now, mentally and physically fit, a business owner, an artist.

A damned good man.

He didn't deserve to be caught up in this mess I had created.

"Did you ever wonder how I made it in rock and roll so

quickly?"

"Of course not," my mom said. "You made it because you're so talented."

Always a mom. Always singing my praises. "Thanks, Mom. I appreciate that."

"She's not blowing smoke up your ass, Jer," Ty said. "Your voice is amazing. It always has been. I used to be jealous as hell of you."

He wouldn't be jealous for long. Pretty soon my big brother would hate me.

"Thanks, Ty. But there are thousands of vocalists in LA, many more talented than I am, who never make it."

"So you got lucky," Mom said. "What's wrong with that?"

"Nothing's wrong with that. But believe me, what happened with Zeb and me isn't that simple." I heaved a sigh. "I met a woman. An heiress. You've probably heard of her. Alicia Hopkins."

"Of course we've heard of her. You were splashed all over the tabloids with her a few years ago. We'd have to be blind not to have noticed."

"Just so you know, there's nothing between Alicia and me." Nothing except nasty sex. Which to me was nothing. Nothing at all.

"Of course, Jeremy," Mom said. "She's way too old for you."

"Too much of a catty bitch for you too," Ty agreed.

How he knew that I had no idea, and I wasn't about to ask questions. Not when I was about to destroy his life.

I cleared my throat. "Zeb and I met up with her and she

made us an offer we couldn't refuse. She funded our entrance into rock and roll, made us into stars, but she asked something in return."

They both stared at me blankly. How could I say this to my mother?

"We had to be at her beck and call for...sex. Whenever she wanted. For as long as she wanted. We could be with whoever we wanted as long as we were there when Alicia called. Which meant we could never fall in love."

My mother went pale.

Tyler touched her arm. "This is not a big deal, Mom. He's talking about LA."

"He's talking about selling his body, Tyler."

I hadn't expected her to take this well. She was my mother, after all. But the worst was yet to come.

"That's the least of it," I said. "She seemed to like me better than Zeb, and she got kind of possessive. When I tried to pull away from our original agreement, she found a way to make sure I never strayed."

"Did she blackmail you?" Tyler asked.

"She did."

"What did she have on you?"

Though I squeezed my eyes shut, a tear ran down my left cheek anyway. Fucking pansy. "She did some digging. She found out about you and Harley Massey, and that I was your alibi. So she dug some more, and she got some high-priced PI to find evidence that you were at Harley's that night."

"What evidence?"

"A hair that was found at the scene. A blond hair."

"She's lying, of course," my mother said.

I shook my head. "She's not. That's not how Alicia operates. I saw the hair strands, and she let me take one of them to a lab for DNA analysis. I gave the lab a lock of my own hair, and asked if the blond hair came from my sibling. I don't need to tell you what the results were."

"She could still be lying. She could have gotten Ty's hair from somewhere else and paid the PI to tell you it was found at Harley's. Wouldn't they have tested the hair after the... incident?"

"No. They wouldn't have thought twice about it because I had an alibi," Tyler said, shaking his head. "None of this is your fault, Jer."

My level-headed brother was a far cry from the crazy-eyed maniac I'd found the night of Harley's death. I'd done the right thing, damn it. I'd given my brother a chance at the life he deserved. He was a good man.

"Ty, I'm not going to let you go down for this. I'm not going to let any of us go down for that piece of sludge Harley Massey. If you hadn't killed him, someone else would have."

"Don't say it like that," my mother said, biting her lip.

She never could use the word kill, or murder, instead calling that night "the incident." My poor mother was about to get a heavy dose of reality if Alicia Hopkins had her way.

"The phone call you got was a warning to me, Mom. A warning to me to stick to my agreement with Alicia, or she'd make the evidence she has public."

They both stared at me, eyes wide, faces pale.

The next words were difficult to say.

"She seems to think I might default. That I won't be her puppet any longer."

"Why would she think that?" my mother asked.

I sighed. "I've met a woman."

CHAPTER THIRTY–SIX

HEATHER

Zane's house was even more ridiculously decadent than Jett's. We didn't spend much time in the house, though, as the party was taking place in his amazing backyard, complete with swimming pool and giant hot tub. A maid quickly led us through the abode and out back.

A table filled with oysters on the half shell and tropical fruit was elaborately set up on his wraparound redwood deck. Men and women alike frolicked naked in the pool and hot tub. And of course there were plenty of women making out in the middle of everything.

A stage was set up, but the band members weren't on it. I spied Bernie Zopes in the hot tub with a blond groupie, but I didn't see Zane or Tony.

Or Jett.

He could be anywhere. Even up in one of what I was sure were myriad bedrooms on the second floor of Zane's mansion.

I couldn't go there. I wanted so much to have faith in what Janet had told me—that Jett was somehow different with me. That he might have true feelings for me.

I'd shared with him a part of me that I hadn't shared with

anyone—something I wasn't sure I'd ever *want* to share with anyone.

I had no regrets. Only sadness that I might never experience anything with Jett again.

Janet and Lindy disrobed quickly and joined in the fun. Susie wasn't quite as eager, but she did remove her red halter top. I'd seen her naked many times. We were roommates, after all. But seeing her breasts bouncing at what was likely to become an all-out orgy freaked me out a little. I really didn't want to witness her having sex. Too weird.

But before I knew it, she pulled on my arm. "Come on! Let's go swimming!"

In barely an instant, she'd shed her shorts and flip-flops and dived into the pool.

Leaving me standing there at the edge, fully clothed, looking like an idiot. Might as well go swimming. My body was as good as the rest of these women's were, *and* it had all original parts.

I bent down to undo the strap on my sandals, and—

"Shit!"

I tumbled into the lukewarm pool, my mouth wide open.

I came up choking as a masculine hand reached toward me. "Babe, I'm so sorry. I didn't mean to bump into you like that."

I took his hand and climbed out of the pool, my clothes dripping wet and my straightened hair already forming those dreaded ringlets that would turn to frizz as soon as they dried.

I hadn't even looked to see who he was when he said, "I'm Zane Michaels."

I looked into his eyes. Yes, he certainly was. Gorgeous Zane Michaels. The ultimate rock pretty boy.

But he was no Jett Draconis.

"Hey, I recognize you," he said. "You're the one Jett jumped off the stage to save the other night."

I opened my mouth to say something, I wasn't sure what, but only a choke came out.

"Hey," he said. "You okay?"

I nodded and cleared my throat. "Just swallowed some water. I'm fine."

"I'm really sorry. Come on into the house. We can put your clothes in the dryer."

He didn't mention what I might wear in the meantime.

I followed him into the house where he led me to the most luxurious laundry room I'd ever seen. It was like a mini laundromat with two industrial frontload washers and two dryers. How much laundry did Zane Michaels have?

"My laundress has the day off, but hopefully I can figure this out."

Apparently enough to employ a "laundress." Was that word even used anymore?

More so than when I'd visited Jett's home, I was now aware of just how much money the members of Emerald Phoenix actually made. Sadness swept through me. This only illuminated the sheer differences between Jett and me. We truly lived in different worlds.

"So where's Jett tonight?" I asked, trying to sound nonchalant.

"Haven't seen him, but I'm sure he's here somewhere.

We're doing a casual concert at midnight, and he knows he needs to be onstage outside a half hour before that." He eyed a clock on the wall. "And that's in fifteen minutes." He stared at me. "So are you going to take your clothes off?"

I wrapped my arms over my chest to hide my hard nipples. "Sure. Do you...have something I could put on?"

"Why? Everyone's naked anyway." He made no move to leave.

"You want me to just undress. Here. In front of you."

"Sugar pie, if you think I can't see your whole body through those wet clothes, think again."

And still, he didn't move.

"I guess I'll just wear wet clothes, then." I turned.

He quickly blocked the door. "Hey, don't be like that. I'll find you something." He sorted through a basket full of laundry, pulled out an Emerald Phoenix T-shirt, and sniffed it. "Smells clean. You can put this on." He held the shirt out to me.

It was big and would probably cover all of me. Good enough. "Now, if I could have a minute of privacy please?"

He chuckled and turned his back. "Sure, babe."

I undressed and put on the T-shirt as quickly as I could since I didn't trust him not to turn around and sneak a peek. Jett spoke highly of him and his talent, but I didn't know the man at all. He didn't turn around, even though his back quivered slightly with what I assumed was laughter.

Asshole.

"Okay," I said once I was safely robed in the T-shirt, which hung halfway to my knees, thank goodness.

He turned and threw my wet clothes into one of the

dryers. "Looks like it'll take about a half hour. Your clothes will be dry in time for our concert, though I warn you, every other woman here will be naked by then."

I couldn't think of anything intelligent or snarky to say to that, so I said nothing.

Didn't matter anyway, because he kept talking.

"You know, I've known Jett a long time, and I've never seen him so enraptured by a woman."

Enraptured? Not really a word I expected to hear out of rocker Zane Michaels's mouth. Classical pianist Zeb Frankfurter's? Maybe.

"Jett told me how you guys went to school together."

"So you know we're well-educated musicians, huh?" He laughed.

"What's so funny about being well-educated musicians?"

"Nothing. Rock and roll is its own kind of art. It's just not what either of us ever thought we'd be doing."

"Do you have regrets?"

"Are you kidding? Look at how I get to live. Hell, no, I don't have regrets. But Jett's another story."

"What do you mean? Does Jett have regrets?"

"Not about getting into rock and roll." He cleared his throat. "Look, I've said too much, but I feel like I should say one more thing." He paused.

Had he changed his mind?

Then, "If Jett decides not to have a relationship with you, it's not because he doesn't want to."

I widened my eyes as tingles erupted all over my still-damp skin. "What do you mean by that?"

"I mean exactly what I said. And that's all I can say."

"Zane, no. That's not fair." After what Janet had said...and now this... Was it truly possible that Jett had feelings for me? And that, for some reason, he couldn't act on them?

Zane moved toward the door. "Sweetie, that's all I can say. And you look fucking hot in my shirt, by the way. If it weren't for Jett, I'd be all over you." He left.

I was oddly flattered by Zane's comment, but more intrigued. From what I knew of Zane Michaels, if he wanted a woman, he went for it. If he wanted me but was leaving me alone because of Jett...

Elation filled me.

I looked up at the clock. Only about a minute until the band would take the stage.

I'd see Jett.

I ran back outside.

Zane, Bernie, and Tony were on the outside stage with a few tech people. They'd all removed their shirts, and their bare chests were sights to behold. Nothing compared to Jett, of course, but still...

"Testing," Zane said into one of the mics. "Hey, J, we're ready to rock and roll! Get over here!"

I looked around, expecting to see Jett push through the crowds to get onstage.

He didn't appear.

People began to chatter, wondering where he was, when a woman forced herself onto the stage and took the mic from Zane.

I gasped. Alicia Hopkins. I hadn't even known she was

here. This certainly wasn't her kind of scene. Or was it? Janet was convinced she had lied to me about Jett staging the bomb threat. Damn. I should have asked Zane about that while we were talking.

She had some kind of strange interest in Jett.

"Ladies and gentlemen," Alicia said into the mic, "I'm sorry to tell you that Jett Draconis won't be performing this evening."

My heart lurched. Was Jett okay?

Huge cries of "Boo!" rose through the air.

"You may not be seeing him for a while," she continued. "Rumor has it that—"

Zane grabbed the mic out of Alicia's hands and he must have turned it off. He spoke to her, and it didn't take a genius to tell from his body language that he was mad as hell.

Alicia rushed off stage.

"No need to worry," Zane said into the mic. "Jett is fine, but unfortunately he's not here this evening. Luckily, I have a pretty darn good set of pipes myself, so I'll be doing the leads and Tony here will take over on lead guitar. You all ready to rock and roll?"

The crowd cheered as the band began.

I walked back into the house and got my clothes out of the dryer. They were still slightly damp, but they'd do. I texted Susie—my phone had survived the pool, thank goodness—to tell her I was leaving and then headed toward the door.

Until a hand grabbed my arm.

I turned and stared straight into Alicia Hopkins's perfectly made-up face.

CHAPTER THIRTY-SEVEN

JETT

"Are you in love?" my mother asked.

I closed my eyes. "Yes. I am."

"And if you begin a relationship with this woman, this other woman will..." My mother sank her head into her hands.

I swallowed—or attempted to—the lump that had formed in my throat. "I won't sacrifice you for anything, Tyler. I promise that. You either, Mom. I won't pursue a relationship with Heather."

"Heather. A beautiful name. What is she like?" My mother asked.

"She's intelligent. And beautiful. And headstrong. And determined. She has a master's in creative writing from Northwestern."

"Sounds perfect for you," Tyler said.

She is. But I didn't say it aloud.

"I have an amazing career, and I have you guys," I said. "I don't need a relationship. You know me. I never saw myself as a husband or a father."

I did now, though. God, did I. I never thought I'd want kids, but the thought of a little girl and little boy with Heather's auburn hair made me feel warm and gooey inside. I'd start them on guitar and piano as soon as their manual dexterity allowed, probably by age five. Maybe one would like to write like Heather. Maybe one would have a singing voice, like I did.

A beautiful fantasy. It would never be my reality.

My brother was saying something, but I hadn't heard it.

"Well, Jeremy?" my mother said.

"I'm sorry. Say that again, Ty."

"Have you tried talking to this Alicia? Can't you reason with her?"

I laughed. "Reason with her? That's not an option, Ty. This is a woman who always gets what she wants and enjoys playing with other people. She does it for sport. She's never had to work a day in her life."

"What if I went out to LA with you," he said. "We could talk to her together."

No way would I put my brother in touch with Alicia. He was doing well, and I wouldn't risk his mental state.

"That's not an option," I said.

"Why not?"

"It's just not," I said with force.

Neither of them questioned me on that again.

"I've arranged for us to see an attorney here in Chicago tomorrow afternoon to talk about options. He comes highly recommended. I have plenty of money and will pay for the best attorneys for all of us. So at least we have that."

"I can't let you go down for something I did," Tyler said. "I can't."

"We *all* did this, Ty," my mother said. "Jeremy agreed to

give you an alibi, and I agreed to keep the whole thing under wraps. We had clear heads when we went into it, and we knew what we were doing. It felt like the right thing at the time."

"I wasn't right in the head. If I had been, I wouldn't have let you do it. Once I got mentally healthy, I considered going to the cops."

"Why didn't you?" I asked.

"*I* wouldn't allow it," Mom said, her eyes protective and feral. "I begged him not to."

I smiled at her and patted her hand. "Hey," I said to Tyler. "I'll never regret it. Look at you now. And we don't know what will happen. It's been almost seven years. It's possible that Alicia is bluffing and won't do anything. If I stay away from Heather, which I will, why would she? And even if she does, maybe the DA won't prosecute. Or maybe the attorney can make a case for self-defense or something." I turned to my mother. "And you're the most innocent in all of this. All you did was keep a secret to protect both of your sons. You most likely won't be prosecuted at all."

"I'd gladly face life in prison to protect both of you," she said.

"We know that, Mom," Tyler said, "but neither of us will ever let that happen."

He was right on that point. If Alicia went rogue, I might not be able to get my brother out of this, but I'd find an attorney who could get my mother off with no more than a slap on the wrist. Then Tyler and I would have to face the consequences of our actions that long-ago night.

I could take it. I had to. My career would wait.

But Tyler? Right now he was mentally fit. I hoped he was strong enough to endure what might be coming.

CHAPTER THIRTY-EIGHT

HEATHER

I yanked my arm out of her grasp. "What do you want?"

"Just a warning, honey. Stay away from Jett."

"Well, he's not here and I am, so I'd say I'm away from him. But I don't really see what business it is of yours if I see him or I don't."

"Everything Jett Draconis does is my business," she hissed. "I made him."

"Yes, I know you helped him make it in rock and roll," I said. "And I'm sure he appreciates it. That doesn't mean he's yours. You didn't give him his musical talent. That's his alone."

"Did he tell you that he fucked me yesterday?" She smiled like a snake.

My heart fell into my stomach with a thud. Tears threatened, but I would not let this witch see me cry. Besides, she could very well be lying. "Who he fucks is his own business. None of mine. And certainly none of yours."

"That's where you're wrong, sweet pea. I *own* him."

"Really? I thought slavery was outlawed a century and a half ago."

She grabbed my arm again. "Don't play superior with me,

you little slut. He's had his fill of you. You're nothing but a fuck to him."

I yanked my arm away once more. "Apparently, that's all you are to him as well. Touch me again, Alicia, and I'll have you arrested for assault and battery."

"Do what you want. My attorneys will make mincemeat out of you."

I didn't respond. I simply walked through the rest of the house and out the door, tears already streaming down my face.

♦ ♦ ♦ ♦

The noon shift.

Better than the evening shift as far as unwanted attention went, but the tips weren't near as good. I inhaled and went to my first table.

Alicia Hopkins? Again?

I wouldn't give her the satisfaction of asking another waitress to cover the table.

"Hello, Alicia. What can I get for you today?"

"Sit down, Heather."

"I'm sorry. I'm working. If you're not going to order anything, I'll help other customers."

"I said sit down. Your manager won't mind. I've already talked to him."

"Well, *I* mind." She didn't need to know that I'd already given my notice and I didn't give a rat's ass what Knox thought about anything. "Let me know when you're ready to order."

I strode over to my next table, took their order, and then took orders for three other tables before Lori Ann, another waitress, tapped me on the shoulder.

"The woman at table seven has complained about you three times to me. Could you take care of her please? She's a pain in the ass."

How well I knew. But Lori Ann was a nice person—a career waitress who had helped me out a lot. I smiled. "Of course."

I walked back to Alicia's table. "What can I get for you today?"

"Your ass in the seat across from me."

What nerve! "Sorry, that's not on the menu, ma'am." I walked away again.

I delivered orders to four other tables and took another order before Knox cornered me. "Take a break, Heather."

"I don't get a break for another three hours. I'm fine."

"Hey, the woman at table seven wants to speak to you, and she just paid me a thousand dollars to make it happen. So go sit there for as long as she wants."

I shook my head. "You're kidding me, right?"

"Do I sound like I'm kidding? That's Alicia Hopkins."

"I know who she is."

"Then you know I'm serious." He handed me a hundred dollar bill. "Here. It's yours if you do it."

"Sorry, Knox. It'll cost you at least half if you want me to talk to that sow."

He rolled his eyes and counted out four more bills. "Fine. Now go see what she wants."

I smiled curtly and placed the bills in the pocket of my apron.

I walked toward Alicia's table, Knox's eyes burning two holes in my back, and then cut an abrupt turn toward the door.

Fuck Knox Jacobson. Fuck Alicia Hopkins.

Fuck two weeks' notice.

I laughed out loud as I crossed the street to catch the bus home.

I was free! Free as a golden eagle flying through the clouds. Free to follow my dream of writing. Just writing. Even if it was a simple blog post. Heck, Julie Powell started out that way by documenting a year of cooking all the recipes in Julia Child's cookbook. I'd find some way to make my writing pay. Determination swept through me like a lightning bolt.

I was also free to figure out what was going on with Jett. Janet and Zane had told me some intriguing things, and I aimed to get to the bottom of everything. If there was any chance I could be with the man I'd fallen in love with, I would find it.

I laughed out loud again.

Stupid Knox Jacobson, taking money to get me to talk to Alicia Hopkins.

I should have demanded the whole thousand.

CHAPTER THIRTY-NINE

JETT

Something jerked me out of a sound sleep.

"Jett, wake up!"

My mother was shaking me. I sat up in bed.

"What is it?"

"It's Ty. He's gone."

"Shit. Really?"

"Yeah. His car is gone. He's not answering his phone."

Damn.

He'd run.

My big brother, who had come so far, had decided to bail.

Why hadn't he come to talk to me? I wasn't going to let him go down. I thought I'd made that clear.

"I'll find him, Mom."

"I'm coming with you."

"No. You need to stay home in case he shows up. Keep your cell on you and call me if you hear anything."

◆ ◆ ◆ ◆

Five hours of searching Chicago, making phone calls, checking with the bus companies and airlines and calling all the hospitals.

And nothing.

I had to go home and tell my mother I'd failed to find her first son.

I'd failed her, and I'd failed Tyler, my big brother.

I'd failed my bandmates by leaving town and skipping the concert at Zane's last night. I'd failed my fans who'd been looking forward to seeing me.

And I'd failed Heather. I couldn't give her what she deserved.

Hell, what we *both* deserved.

I'd most likely be going to prison along with my brother. I'd take time if I had to in order to get my mother off the hook.

Failure.

A long time had passed since I'd used that word to describe myself. But I couldn't even take credit for my success. That credit belonged to Alicia.

Fucking Alicia.

She would ruin me and my family, and she'd laugh as she did it. I did have one consolation, though. I'd never have to go near the bitch again. I'd no longer have to come when she called, stick my dick into her evil body.

As glad as that thought made me, I'd gladly fuck her for the rest of my life if I could save Tyler and my mom.

But could I give up Heather? Heather, who had grown to be as necessary to me as breathing?

I drove up to Mom's house and went inside.

She ran up to me, her eyes pleading.

"I'm sorry," I said. "I couldn't find him."

"Oh, Jeremy!" She fell into my arms, sobbing. "He was doing so well."

"I know. I know. But this is all on me, Mom."

"No. Don't say that."

"If I hadn't been so eager to make it to the top..." I shook my head and kissed the top of my mother's hair. "I'm so sorry."

"Not your fault," she said again, the words muffled by her soft weeping.

We stood there, hugging, for what seemed like an eternity, until the door opened.

"Mom. Jer."

My mom gasped and pulled away from me. "Tyler!" She ran into my brother's arms.

I turned and stared. An attractive woman in a navy blue suit accompanied him.

"Ty," I said. "Where have you been? We've been worried sick."

"I know. And I'm sorry. But I have a lot to tell you both." He turned to the woman. "This is Fran O'Hara. She's a friend of mine. And an attorney."

Fran held out her hand to Mom. "It's good to meet you, Mrs. Gustafson."

"Call me Eden," Mom said. "But I'm afraid I don't understand—"

"She's *our* attorney, Mom," Tyler said. "I just hired her."

"I've known Tyler for a couple years," Fran said. "He made all the furniture for my office."

"Fran was good enough to see me this morning without an

appointment," Tyler said. "In fact, she cleared her schedule for the day at my request."

"Whatever for?" I asked.

"Fran specializes in criminal defense," Tyler said.

My stomach churned. "Tyler. What have you done?"

"Something I should have done a long time ago. Can we sit down, please?"

Tyler led us all into the living room, where he sat with Fran on the couch, and Mom and I each took a chair.

"I've made a deal," Tyler said. "Or rather, Fran made an amazing deal for me. I should let her tell it."

"Tyler explained to me what happened with Harley Massey," she said. "How you both helped him cover up his involvement."

Nausea swept up my throat as fingers of fear clawed at me. I didn't like where this was going.

"I called the DA," Fran continued, "who happens to be a law school classmate of mine. I explained the situation, and we were able to strike a deal."

"What deal?" Mom asked, her voice shaking.

Tyler cleared his throat. "I'm probably going to prison."

"No!" Mom stood.

"Sit down, Mom," I said, my body numb. "Let's hear him out."

"I have to do it," Tyler said. "I should have done it seven years ago. I'm guilty, after all."

"But of course there are many extenuating circumstances," Fran said. "And luckily the DA understands that. What Tyler did amounts to voluntary manslaughter, not murder. The DA thinks he can get the judge to accept a guilty plea to the lesser crime of involuntary manslaughter with a sentence not to exceed twelve months in prison."

I swallowed the lump in my throat, feeling numb. "What if the judge *doesn't* accept that?"

"Then I go to trial for voluntary manslaughter, Jer. It's okay. I know the risk involved."

"But this is an old crime," Fran said. "The judge will probably be thrilled to plead it down. The dockets are overflowing. Plea bargains happen all the time. It's standard procedure."

"No, Ty," Mom said. "You can't go to prison. I won't allow it."

"With all due respect, Mom, that's not your decision to make. I'm a grown man."

"There's more," Fran said. "My deal with the DA includes immunity for both of you. Neither of you will be prosecuted as accessories after the fact."

"No," Mom said again. "You can't do this, Ty."

"I can do this, and I will. You two have always been there for me, and now Jeremy is in a mess because of what he did to help me." He turned to me. "You deserve love, bro. Go find your woman. Tell her how you feel."

"Ty—"

"Hey, you want me to put you in the dryer again?"

I couldn't help a chuckle. When I was two, apparently I'd done something to piss Ty off—he couldn't remember what— and he'd put me in the dryer. I didn't remember any of it, but Mom and Ty told the story all the time.

"Let me do this for you, Jer. I owe you, brother." He patted his left upper arm.

Though his long-sleeved button-down hid it, I knew what he was referencing. Before I left for LA, Ty and I had gotten matching Celtic lion tattoos—a nod to our mother's Irish heritage, and also a celebration of our brotherhood. We'd always be there for each other no matter what, no matter where life led either of us. I choked up a little, not able to respond.

"I'll be okay. I'm on my meds, and twelve months is a long cry from forever."

"But if they don't accept the plea—"

"Then I go to trial. And with Fran here representing me, I might just get off."

"I assure you that you're worrying needlessly," Fran said. "There's a ninety-nine percent chance the judge will accept the plea."

Mom finally backed down, nodding. "All right, Ty. If you're sure."

"I'm sure, Mom. Let me clean up my own mess for once."

"When do you see the judge?" I asked.

"I was able to call in a favor and get him on the docket for four this afternoon." She checked her watch. "Which means we need to get to the courthouse."

"We'll all go," I said. "I should change. But I don't have a suit here at home."

"Just something other than jeans will be fine," Fran said.

I stood and shook Fran's hand. "Just so you know, don't worry about getting your bills paid. I'll take care of all of it."

"I wasn't worried. I told Ty I'd be happy to take it in a

bedroom suite for my new home." She smiled.

"One way or the other, you'll get every penny and then some," I assured her. Then I went to my room to change.

CHAPTER FORTY

HEATHER

Though I was tempted to blow it on Rodeo Drive, the five hundred dollars I'd gotten from Knox went straight into the bank. I had a nice savings, but who knew how frugally I'd have to live until I found a way to make decent money from my writing? I had enough to live on for about a year if I didn't earn anything at all, so that gave me a goal. I had to get something going within a year.

I was going to do it.

I hadn't heard from Jett, and I was still a little worried that he hadn't shown up for Zane's party the prior evening. As much as I loved him, though, I hated the fact that he was somehow bound to Alicia Hopkins.

I made myself a grilled ham and cheese sandwich for dinner, poured a glass of Sauvignon Blanc, and set up my laptop on the kitchen table to start my research on freelance writing. I was willing to do anything.

By nine o'clock, I had some good ideas percolating, and I set up a blog called *Heather's Haven.* Kind of cheesy, but what the heck? No one would be reading it for a while anyway. I had a friend down the hall who was a tech geek, so I'd get her to help me with search optimization and all the other stuff I didn't understand. I shot her a quick email and then rose to refill my wine glass.

A knock on the door startled me. It was a weeknight, and I rarely got visitors when Susie wasn't home. I hoped it wasn't Janet or Lindy trying to invite me to another wild party. As much as I honestly liked the two of them as people, that just was not my scene.

Nope. Now I was a writer. A true "I write for a living" writer. I had a career to work on. I was ready to spend every spare minute making this work. No more parties. No more dead-end jobs.

I opened the door—

"Oh!"

Jett stood there, wearing casual black Dockers and a tan cotton shirt, the top few buttons undone, his chest hair peeking out. His dark hair was pulled back in a messy Brock O'Hurn-style man bun.

And he was smiling.

"Hi, J—"

He crushed his lips to mine. I opened for him without thinking. God, his kiss. How had I ever thought I could live without those kisses? We kissed deeply for a few timeless moments until he broke it with a loud smack of suction. His eyes were dark and filled with lust.

He walked into my apartment and pushed the door shut, trapping me against the wall. He slammed his lips down onto mine once more while he slid one hand up my side to cup my breast. My nipple hardened instantly, and he thumbed it gently through my camisole.

I strained forward, wanting to touch every part of me to every part of him.

His torture of my nipple became more urgent as he twisted it through the silky fabric. I moaned into his mouth, pushing myself against his hardness. I slid a hand from around his neck to the band holding his man bun in place. I tugged, releasing his hair and threading my fingers through the softness.

The need to feel his muscles, his skin, soared through me, and I unbuttoned his shirt quickly and brushed it over his shoulders. My breath caught at his beauty. I fingered the majestic lion on his left upper arm, his skin warm beneath my fingertips.

I slid my other hand down his hard chest to his black pants. I unbuckled his belt and unzipped his fly, releasing his glorious cock.

He groaned when I fisted him, pulling my hand toward his head and then swirling my finger through the drop of fluid and around his cockhead.

He broke our kiss and pushed me to my knees. "Suck my cock, Heather."

Gladly. I licked the precome from his glistening head, savoring the saltiness. Then I plunged onto him, letting his head nudge the back of my throat.

"Oh, God, baby," he rasped. "Can't take it. Need you." He pulled me toward him. "Take off your shorts. Quickly."

I obeyed, and he lifted me in his strong arms and set me on his hard cock. My back was braced against the wall as he thrust into me. My nipples strained through my camisole, aching for his touch, abrading against the silky fabric.

And he thrust.

And he thrust.

And he thrust.

"Heather"—*thrust*—"Heather"—*thrust*—"Fuck. Heather."

He filled every part of me, even the emptiest most inner parts of my soul.

My orgasm crept up quickly, and I exploded around him, crying out in loud moans.

"That's right, baby. Come all over me. That's ri— Fuck!" He thrust into me, my shoulder hitting a nail in the wall and nicking me, but I didn't care. It all added to the profuse pleasure skyrocketing through me as the man I loved fucked me into oblivion.

The man I loved...

He had come to me.

Come back for me.

He leaned against me, his breath loud and heavy in my ear for a few moments before he spoke.

"Heather," he said huskily, "I have to know. Did you hear me the other night? The last time we were together?"

My body thrummed with desire. What was he talking about? "What?" I choked out.

"I said something to you. Something serious. You didn't respond."

"I'm...sorry, Jett. I don't remember anything unusual."

"Jeremy, damn it. Call me Jeremy."

"Okay. Jeremy."

"I said I loved you, Heather. I fucking said I loved you, and you didn't respond."

My knees wobbled, and he grabbed my arm to steady me.

"You l-love me?" I whispered.

"I thought I felt something from you too. Thought I saw it in your eyes, but when you didn't respond—"

"Oh my God. I love you too. I love you so much!" I hurled myself back into his arms.

How had I missed a declaration of love?

"Thank God," he said against my hair. "I was so afraid—"

I pulled away. "I'm so sorry I didn't hear it. I never thought...in a million years... You seemed so unattainable. You've had so many women. You could have whomever you want."

"I want *you*, Heather. Only you."

"Oh my God." I sighed.

"I haven't led the most virtuous life. I know that. But is there any way you might be able to—"

I pressed my fingertips to his lips. "I love you. I had to push it aside because I didn't think you could possibly... How could anyone *not* love you?"

He smiled slightly. "No one has ever loved me, other than my mother and my brother. Not the way I want to be loved."

"You know that's not true. Your fans love you."

"They love Jett. I want to be loved as Jeremy."

"Well, I love you both. Jett is part of Jeremy, and you're both wonderful. You did something amazing for me."

"Oh?" He waggled his eyebrows.

"Something other than that. When I met you, I had decided to quit writing, to give up on my dream. You convinced me not to."

"I did?"

"You did. Your love of music and your drive to succeed however you could... It really moved me. I quit the diner, and I've been working on ways to make my writing pay. I may not be writing for the big screen now, but I can write other things. I can still pursue my love. That's because of you."

"I think that's the nicest thing anyone has ever said to me, Heather. God, I love you."

"And I love you. With my whole heart, my whole soul."

He smiled. "And with that beautiful body of yours?"

"Whenever you want. But what about Alicia? She told me to stay away from you."

"Screw Alicia," he said. "Alicia doesn't matter anymore."

"Works for me." I fingered his tattoo. "I've always wondered about this. It's beautiful work."

"I got it before I left for LA. My brother got the same one. It was... This might sound corny to you."

"No it won't. I think it's wonderful that you and your brother are close."

"We are. But the tattoo means more. There's a lot I need to tell you about that. And you may change your mind about me."

"I won't," I said. "I know about Alicia."

"You know she helped me. What you don't know is that—"

"You fucked her a few days ago." The words popped out of my mouth. "She told me."

"She's a known liar, but I *have* fucked her many times. It meant nothing to me. As for a few days ago, she only *thinks*

232

I fucked her. I actually blindfolded her and used a dildo. I couldn't get hard for her, Heather. I despise her. But even without the despising, I'm not sure I can ever get hard for another woman again. You're all I want."

His words warmed me, and I cupped his crotch.

Granite met my palm.

"Exhibit A," he said. "I just had you, and you've got me hard again."

I couldn't help a sly smile.

But he pushed my hand away and buttoned his pants. "I have to tell you some stuff first. News is going to come out about me and my family. My career might take a hit, though I've already got my publicity team on it."

"What kind of news?"

He cleared his throat. "I'm just going to come right out with it. I gave my brother an alibi seven years ago when he inadvertently killed a man."

I clamped my hand to my mouth.

"It was an accident, and there were extenuating circumstances. But Alicia found out about it and has been blackmailing me for the last several years to keep me under her thumb."

"She's even more of a bitch than I thought," I said.

"She's a miserable human being," he said. "But she's irrelevant now. My brother went to the DA and he cut a deal. I'm not in any trouble, and I owe my brother everything."

"Sounds like maybe you owe each *other* everything."

He smiled, running his fingers lightly over the lion on his upper arm. "You're wonderful. Do you know that?"

"No more wonderful than you are, especially to save your brother the way you did."

"It's a long story," he said, "but we have all night. You want another glass of wine?"

I smiled. "Later. Like you said, we have all night. Right now I want you to take me to bed. I want to make love with the man I'm hopelessly in love with."

"I want that too, baby. For the rest of our lives." He swooped me into his arms, and we headed into my bedroom.

ALSO AVAILABLE FROM

HELEN HARDT

Unchained

from

The Blood Bond Saga

Coming Soon
Keep reading for an excerpt!

EXCERPT FROM
UNCHAINED

DANTE

Lust rolled through me. I stood against a sink in the men's room where Erin—that's what the other guy had called her—had pushed me, and I glanced in the mirror.

My jaw dropped. I looked like a wild man, my hair in disarray, several days' growth of dark beard on my jawline, blood drying on my cheeks and chin. But that in itself wasn't what astounded me. The last time I'd seen my reflection, an eighteen-year-old high school student had stared back at me. Now I was looking at a man's jaw, a man's profile, a man's beard. The skin around my eyes showed slight signs of age, a few wrinkles here and there. My front teeth no longer had a gap between them. They'd moved together somehow. Maybe when my wisdom teeth had erupted. I remembered the pain when they broke through my gums, pain that had seemed like nothing after what I'd been through.

So long ago now...as if they were only fuzzy memories from a dream. *Or a nightmare.*

Still, I was a mess. I was lucky she hadn't run screaming. Instead, she was trying to help me. Help I didn't deserve after desecrating her blood bank. Who was she? And why hadn't she responded to my attempt to glamour her?

Her scent had intoxicated me. She was one of *them*—the humans with dark hair and fair skin, whose blood tasted better than the most exotic nectar. Her eyes were a light green, almost as light as a peridot, and they sparkled with fire and ice simultaneously.

My gums began to tingle once more. Just the thought of Erin's blood awakened my urge to feed.

I'd gorged on the bagged blood, enough that I should have been sated. I couldn't go back for more. Someone would have been notified to clean up by now.

More bagged blood wouldn't help anyway. I wanted *her* blood.

I tried to push the hunger from my mind and concentrate on something more important.

I was free.

Unchained from the shackles that had bound me for so many years.

So why did I still feel like I was imprisoned?

I was still in New Orleans. Was my family still here? Dad? Em? River? Uncle Braedon? Grandpa Bill? Bill might be over a hundred years old by now. He could very well be gone.

Even if they *were* still here, I had no idea how to get in touch with them.

Erin. Erin was my only chance.

What if she forgot? Didn't come back for me?

I resisted the urge to lick the dried blood from my face

and hands—it wouldn't satisfy me anyway—and furiously scrubbed at them.

Erin.

I needed her blood. I needed *her*.

I'd felt it. She needed something from me as well. I wasn't sure what, but I'd felt the tug. She wanted to touch me. Couldn't stop herself from putting her hand on my skin, even though I must have looked like an animal after a kill with blood streaming from my lips.

I'd brushed her away, for fear I'd lose the last thread of self-control keeping me from lunging toward her, sinking my teeth into her soft flesh, and taking from her the sustenance I craved.

Hunger still clawed at me. Not just for Erin's blood, but for Erin herself. My groin tightened.

Not again.

I willed the erection down. Couldn't go there. Not now. I'd had erections during captivity and no way to release, with my hands always bound. I certainly had no way to release now. How long had I been gone? I had no idea. Only that it had been years. Many, many years.

Erin had told me to stay put, that she'd come back for me. Could I trust her? Why would she want to help me?

I had to get out of here. If I stayed in one place for too long, I risked being tracked by *her*. Vampires had no scent to each other, but we had other ways of keeping tabs. I had no doubt *she* had the ability to find me.

I grasped the edge of the sink, steadying myself.

★ ★ ★ ★

I pulled against the leather restraints. "Who the hell are you? Why am I here?"

The woman was dazzling...in a terrifying way. She was masked, except for her icy blue eyes. When she smiled, her fangs were already long and sharp.

"Don't you recognize your queen, Dante?"

She was delusional. We recognized the government of the places we lived. In this case, the United States of America, which didn't have a queen.

My clothes were gone. I lay naked, my wrists and ankles shackled to a table. Or was it a bed?

"So young and beautiful. I can smell the testosterone flowing through you, turning your boy's body into a man's. How old are you? Sixteen? Seventeen?"

I was eighteen. A late bloomer, something I found pretty embarrassing. My cousin, River, who was a month younger than I, had matured before I had. My voice had finally changed two years ago, which was the signal that a male vampire had become fertile.

"You are no queen," I said through clenched teeth. "Let me go."

She laughed. "You will recognize me as your queen soon enough."

"Let me go!" I demanded once more. "My father will come for me. My uncle. My grandfather. They are more powerful than you could ever hope to be."

She snarled, her fangs bared. "They're already on their

way, sweet one. Something I was counting on."

★ ★ ★ ★

A thud pulled me out of the nightmare.

I'd fallen to the hard tile floor.

That horrible night, so long ago, when I'd awakened in her dungeon.

Escape. I needed to flee *now*. Erin had promised to help, but I couldn't wait. Not when *she* could already be on my trail. I left the men's room with my face and hands now clean, but my clothes were a different matter. They were tattered—they'd come from a homeless man, after all—and covered in blood. I sneaked down a hallway until I found a locker room. I traded what I was wearing for a pair of jeans that were slightly small on me and a black hoodie. I didn't like stealing, but I had no choice.

I raced around, looking for the back door where I'd entered.

No! A pull. Erin was mentally tugging me toward something. Something I'd seen before.

I ambled into the emergency room, trying to look inconspicuous, when something tight wrapped around my wrist, and I flinched. I rubbed at it, but found only the calluses from the leather bindings I had finally left behind.

Then I saw it.

A man on a gurney had grabbed *Erin's* wrist. The need to protect her hurled into me like a cyclone. I inhaled, yet I smelled only Erin's scent. But I recognized the man.

"Why won't he let go?" Erin asked, pleading.

"I don't know." A woman in a white coat was looking into the man's eyes with a flashlight or something. "Pupils are dilated. We need to take some blood for a drug panel."

I knew what to do. I quickly walked toward the gurney and gazed into the homeless man's eyes, letting go of the glamour that had been holding the homeless man since I'd run from the cop earlier. In my hurry to get away, I hadn't released him.

The doctor was too involved in her work to notice me, but when the man closed his eyes and let go of Erin's hand, she looked up.

"You!" she said.

I turned and walked swiftly toward the first door I could find.

This story continues in
Unchained
from Helen Hardt's Blood Bond Saga!

ACKNOWLEDGMENTS

I've always fantasized about being a rock star, and I still love covering Joan Jett and Chrissie Hynde on karaoke nights. Living in that world for this fictional party was a lot of fun!

Many thanks to my editor, Celina Summers, my line editor, Scott Saunders, and my proofreaders, Lia Fairchild, Jessica Robinson, and Chrissie Saunders. You all know how to make my work shine, and it's always better for your efforts.

Thank you to Meredith, Jon, and David at Waterhouse Press for asking me to write in this series, and to the rest of the Waterhouse team—Robyn, Yvonne, Jesse, Kurt, Haley, Jeanne, and Jennifer—for doing your part.

Most of all, thank you to my street team, Hardt and Soul, and to all my other readers. I hope you have as much fun reading Misadventures with a Rock Star as I had writing it!

ALSO AVAILABLE FROM
WATERHOUSE PRESS

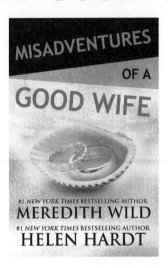

Kate and Price Lewis had the perfect marriage—love, fulfilling careers, and a great apartment in the city. But when Price's work takes him overseas and his plane goes down, their happily-ever-after goes down with it.

A year later, Kate is still trying to cope. She's tied to her grief as tightly as she was bound to Price. When her sister-in-law coaxes her into an extended girls' trip—three weeks on a remote island in the South Pacific—Kate agrees. At a villa as secluded as the island, they're the only people in sight, until Kate sees a ghost walking toward them on the beach. Price is alive.

Their reunion is anything but picture perfect. Kate has been loyal to the husband she thought was dead, but she needs answers. What she gets instead is a cryptic proposal—go back home in three weeks, or disappear with Price...forever.

Emotions run high, passions burn bright, and Kate faces an impossible choice. Can Price win back his wife? Or will his secrets tear them apart?

Visit Misadventures.com for more information!

ALSO AVAILABLE FROM
WATERHOUSE PRESS

I've spent my life in a cage, cloistered by politics and social maneuvering. A prisoner to expectation. Yet I'd give anything to be a certain man's slave.

A year ago, I wouldn't have recognized the woman I've become. That was before I discovered Crave. Before Demitri ripped the inhibitions clean off my body the first time he undressed me with his icy blue eyes in the club that fateful night.

Now he's all I can think about. I can't breathe until he makes me his. Except he won't take me until he breaks me. And I'm not an easy submissive to break.

Visit Misadventures.com for more information!

MORE MISADVENTURES

VISIT MISADVENTURES.COM
FOR MORE INFORMATION!

MORE MISADVENTURES

**VISIT MISADVENTURES.COM
FOR MORE INFORMATION!**